Heavier Than Air

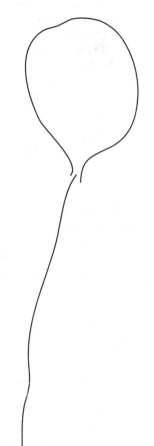

NONA CASPERS

heavier than air

University of
Massachusetts
Press
Amherst and
Boston

This book is the winner of the 2005 Grace Paley Prize for Short Fiction.
The Association of Writers & Writing Programs, which sponsors the award, is a
national nonprofit organization dedicated to serving American letters, writers,
and programs of writing. Its headquarters are at George Mason University, Fairfax,
Virginia, and its website is www.awpwriter.org.

Copyright © 2006 by University of Massachusetts Press

Printed in the United States of America

LC 2006023897

ISBN 10: 1-55849-556-8
ISBN 13: 978-1-55849-556-2

Designed by Kristina Kachele Design, LLC
Set in Quadraat with Sansa Soft Display by dix!
Printed and bound by the Maple-Vail Book Manufacturing Group, Inc.

Library of Congress Cataloging-in-Publication Data

Caspers, Nona.
   Heavier than air / Nona Caspers.
       p.   cm.
   "Winner of the Association of Writers and Writing Programs
Grace Paley Prize in Short Fiction."
ISBN-13: 978-1-55849-556-2 (cloth : alk. paper)
ISBN-10: 1-55849-556-8 (cloth : alk. paper)
   1. Middle West—Social life and customs—Fiction.
I. Title.
PS3553.A79523H43   2006
813'.54—dc22
                 2006023897

British Library Cataloguing in Publication data are available.

It's too big you know—I mean life sir.

—L. S. Lowry, 1961

Acknowledgments

The following stories have been previously published, some in slightly different form. "Country Girls" in The Iowa Review; "Mr. Hellerman's Vacation" in The Ontario Review; "The EE Cry" (under the title "Fat") and "Mother" in The Cimarron Review; "Vegetative States" and "Wide Like an Eagle's Wings" in Fourteen Hills; "Vegetative States" in Hers[2] (Faber and Faber); "Heavier Than Air" in Literal Latte; "Alfalfa" in CALYX and Women on Women (Plume); "La Maison de Madame Durard" in Hers[3].

The author gratefully acknowledges support from the Barbara Deming Memorial Fund, the Joseph Henry Jackson Literary Grant and Award, and San Francisco State University. She also thanks the AWP and the University of Massachusetts Press. She thanks the following people for more than is obvious: Barbara Tomash, Toni Mirosevich and Shotsi Faust, Laine Snowman, Toni Graham, Shelley Gage, Ellen Thompson, Margi Dunlap, Jane Meredith Adams, Hillary Seldon-Illick, Michelle Carter, Molly Giles, Maxine Chernoff, Susan Harper, Kris Sayre, Tami Spector, the Caspers clan, and Elaine Buckholtz.

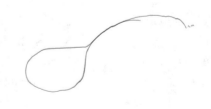

Contents

Heavier Than Air

Country Girls

THE PICTURE on the cover of the dairy magazine was of a middle-aged farm woman, about forty, smiling directly, yet shyly, into the camera. She wore five blue ribbons around her neck. Her skin was clear, almost translucent, and her eyes were lovely and innocent, not the innocence of the religious devout or a child—she was a grown woman—but the sure-footed innocence of a herdswoman. The woman in the picture was once my friend—that is why my father sent the magazine—and for a moment I felt transported against my will back to my parents' home, the air too thin, the rooms too small, me pacing the short hallway from my bedroom to the living room window, and I felt a wave of the deepest longing I had ever known, a longing too large for the body, almost cartoonish unless you are the one living it, and you are fourteen, and then it is deathly serious.

In the spring of 1974, my parents moved from Saint Cloud, Minnesota, where we had been living since I was born, to a dairy farm north of Melrose near Cedar Lake. My father had been hired as the

Melrose County Dairy Cow Inspector and Milk Tester. My mother, who had grown up in the area, didn't want to live in town so they rented a beat-up farmhouse on the land her sister and her family farmed. My parents had planned to move in the summer so my brothers and I could finish our school year, but I had been unhappy in the junior high in Saint Cloud, skipping classes and drinking, and my parents decided not to wait but to pull me out of school for the rest of the year, which was partly a relief. They left my two older brothers behind with the parents of friends.

For the first time in my life I spent a lot of time alone, walking through the unplanted black fields and semiwooded pastures around our new house. Mornings I would hike deep into the pasture in my rubber boots and dig up cow bones, which I hauled back in paper grocery sacks. I stacked the bones up against the back of the house. On warm afternoons I sat back there in my sweatshirt and bandanna, painting the skulls, jaws, and femurs bright psychedelic colors, oranges and purples. In the back of my mind I thought I'd send them to my friends in Saint Cloud. I laid the bones on the grass to dry, the colors clashing with the quiet yellows and greens of the countryside.

One afternoon I hiked across the barley field, down a short hill that led to Adley Creek. I sat on the yellow grass and smoked a Kool. Adley Creek cut through the meadow and divided the land that came with our house from the rest of my Aunt Katie's farm. Aunt Katie was my mother's sister. She and her three kids were farming both parts and I knew they planned to keep some of their dairy herd in our empty barn. I took a long drag on my cigarette and blew out smoke rings, something I had learned to do in the parking lot at school. The rings floated up and as I watched one I saw across the creek a girl with long gold hair. She was standing perfectly still with both arms at her sides examining a fence. She walked over to the wire fence and shook it, bent down and fiddled with the bottom wire. A heifer walked up to her and she grabbed a handful of its neck and pushed the cow away. Not in a mean way, but with a sense of authority.

A few days later, on a Sunday morning, I was eating breakfast with my mother and father at the kitchen table when my Aunt Katie pulled up our gravel driveway in her pickup. From the table we could see her jump out with a basket wrapped in a dishtowel. She wore a plaid wool coat open over jeans and she moved like someone who had been up and working for hours. She knocked on our kitchen door and walked in.

"Yackety yack," my father said and moved his hand like a lobster claw as he reached for another one of my mother's homemade rolls. Though he didn't dislike Aunt Katie, he usually pretended he did—perhaps on the mere principle that talking was a vice, something that should be contained, or perhaps because he liked her too much.

"You don't need to be so critical of me already," Katie said. She plopped the basket on the table. "It's eggs and I would have been over sooner but we've had a horrible flu, and if one of the kids isn't throwing up it's another. The one out there still has the fever but she's got a hard head and wouldn't stay home." She turned to me and shook her finger. "I suppose because she wants to see Miss At-The-Crick here. You stay away from her, though, or you'll be the next one heaving your guts out."

I was grateful that my aunt had not told my parents what I was doing at the creek and looked away from the table out the window. From where I sat I could see the girl in the passenger side of the truck. She was sitting quietly staring at our house. I had not seen Auntie Katie's kids for two years, which felt like a long time to me; I could barely remember one from the other, except they were shy and spoke with German accents like my aunt and like my mother, only my mother's accent had faded from living in the city. The girl got out and stood next to the truck. She was dressed a lot like Aunt Katie: blue jeans and a thin plaid coat, not wool but cotton and one of the pockets was ripped out. She was dragging the heel of her tennis shoe in the dirt.

"Can I just say hi?" I asked.

My mother nodded.

"Stand upwind to avoid germs," my father said.

I went out the kitchen door and through the garage. It was chilly out and I was still in my pajamas. She looked up from dragging her heel and stuck one hand in her coat pocket and the other in her jeans pocket. She had thick, long, gold hair, not yellow gold but dark gold like oat stems or rope. She looked like Aunt Katie, high cheekbones in a flat oval face and wide green-blue eyes. A chill shot through me and I rubbed my arms.

"How come you have your nightclothes on?" she asked me.

"Just woke up."

She laughed as if I'd told a joke.

"No, I'm serious. I just woke up. What time did you get up?"

She shrugged. "We milk at six."

She was the only girl my age I'd seen for weeks and I wanted to impress her the way I had impressed kids in Saint Cloud, mainly by bullshitting or by guzzling moonshine and jumping over fires at quarry parties outside town. Cynthia was shy but eerily self-possessed; she gave the feeling of grass or wheat or stone. I know now that these qualities are not entirely unusual for farm girls, especially those who worked the land as much as Cynthia did, but at that time she seemed like a rare and haunting creature.

"Want to see my skulls?" I asked. "I'm going to send them to my friends in Saint Cloud."

She nodded. I brought her around the side of the house to the back where my metal chair sat facing out toward the barley field. Her eyes got big and she took a step back, as if I'd shown her dead bodies themselves.

I had laid the painted bones out on the patches of dirt and grass that went up the field. Now I walked around them and picked out one purple skull with orange eye sockets. I held it up to her.

"Here," I said. "You can have one."

She kept her hands in her pockets and looked at the ground.

"Maybe you want to paint one," I said.

She shook her head.

"Why not?"

"I like them plain, like these." She picked out a long femur from my stack against the house and she squatted and dragged the tip of the bone through a patch of dirt.

"I have two milking cows," she said.

I looked at her to see if she was serious. She gazed up at me with a face plain and straightforward. I threw the orange painted bone high up over the field and watched it drop. I could feel her watching me so I threw another one. The bone sailed over the yard, over the field, and landed in the dirt. I looked back at her but she looked away. My Aunt Katie walked up from the side of the house.

"Looks like you've been cleaning the fields," she said. "Time to hit the road," she nudged Cynthia, who laid the bone back where she'd found it and smiled at me.

That evening my mother told me that Cynthia had had some trouble in school early on learning to read but that she had a knack for fixing things, fences, broken carts, machinery. She also had a knack for animal husbandry and was starting her own chickens and a dairy herd. Back at my old school, I would have thought this was ridiculous; my friends and I would have joked about it. But that night, from my bed, I kept wondering what my mother would say I had a knack for, besides getting drunk. I looked out my window at the still grass, the wheat, the sky, and instead of feeling trapped or bored I felt a quiet excitement, a new kind of racing inside me. I closed my eyes and saw Cynthia's wide, green-blue eyes.

Monday morning I rode along with my father on his work route. This was part of my rehabilitation, but I liked it. My father sat in his big white truck and counted silos as he drove from farm to farm and gleaned samples of unpasteurized milk from the galvanized tanks in the milk rooms. He inserted a thin, sterile hose into the tank and filled small glass tubes with milk. He also sampled individual cows when they had sores, patches of missing fur, or what my father called swells. Then he labeled and stacked the tubes in a metal tray and placed them in a stainless steel refrigerator half full of dry ice in the back of the truck. At the end of the day he delivered the samples to the laboratory in Sauk Centre where they were tested for quality of protein, unusual bacteria, and infectious viruses.

While my father set up his equipment, I would pull on my black rubber boots and walk up and down the stalls writing down the tag numbers for his records and noting any cows that had signs of infection or illness. Then I'd step outside the barn to see if any cows were what my father called "acting strange" in the pasture. Sometimes, if the farmer came out and they got to talking, I'd kick around the barn—climb up into the hayloft or pet the calves, running the flat of my hand from their nose to the groove between their ears.

On the first day I had gone out with my father I saw Alquin Schultz, a tall, thin man with a sorrowful face, leaning over a cow in the barn and talking quietly into that groove, as if he were telling the cow secrets. Then that same week my mother told me his wife had moved out of their house and in with a mechanic in Sauk Centre. "People get carried away with themselves," my mother said, with little sympathy for either party, though she was not a harsh woman.

At the end of the day I asked my father to stop at Aunt Katie's farm. We pulled up in the drive just as the sun went behind their barn, which softened the air. My dad went into the house but I stayed outside. Most of the herd lay in a clump far away under the shade of an elm tree, but in a separate corral behind the barn stood two half-grown heifers. They looked different from the rest of Aunt Katie's herd; they had black faces and solid white bodies except for spots of black on their legs. They reminded me of panda bears. And they were clean: no bits of dirt and manure crusted on their haunches and tails, no fur coarse with dust.

I climbed on the corral fence and watched the cows watch me. In a little while I heard the house door open and close and Cynthia walked up to the fence where I sat. As soon as she stood near me, my breath calmed, as if the water and bone and air inside me were mirroring the dirt and sky outside.

"These are Black-faced Angus, here," she said, putting her hands on top of the fence and giving it a shake. "Eda and Classic. Most of my mom's herd is Holsteins, which are easy milkers but so are Angus. You can go in there if you want."

The hay in the pen was fresh. Cynthia went into the barn and came back with a bucket and two brushes. "You go like this," she said, and gave Classic two hard strokes up her side against the fur line and then a long softer stroke down.

I started brushing Eda. Short white hairs spun up into my nose. The cows stood still as rocks, except every once in a while they'd twitch and a white ripple would cross their backs as if a snake were running under their hides. And they were warm. Cynthia showed me how to groom their legs and backside and tails, and I built up a sweat that made my skin itch under my bra and my face go hot, which felt good against the cooling evening air.

"This here," Cynthia said, patting the cow between the ears in the deepest part of the groove. "Is its soft spot. Just like a baby's. Once I seen a farmer get mad and hit a cow hard in that spot and the cow dropped over dead in an instant." She stared at me. I put my hand on top of her hand. My arms were thin and freckled like my father's and Cynthia's arms were thick and white like the bones.

"That's where the farmers' secrets go," I said, and then I moved my hand from the cow's head to Cynthia's head where the groove would be and pressed down. Cynthia gripped my shoulders and wheeled me away from Classic's sudden step forward.

"She don't like that," she said.

Holding me in front of her, she looked at me for what seemed like a long time, though it was probably only a few seconds. She looked at me the way no one had or has ever looked at me since— with unabashed curiosity and attention.

"You are Nora Schneider," she said.

"Nora," my father called from his truck, smiling. "Daylight's burning."

My mother was standing by the stove talking with Katie on the phone when we got home. The table was set with fried potatoes, sausage, green beans. She hung up and gave my father a look that meant food's cold, but also something else, a buried hurt or resentment. Though I believe my parents loved each other and that my father was faithful, I also know that on occasion he became smitten with other women. Once, about six months before we'd moved, I overheard my mother on the phone say "his mind's drifting into something again." During these times, my father would stay up late and pace the house; sometimes he'd sleep in a chair in the living room.

There was a towel draped over my mother's shoulder and now she pulled it off and used it to lift a covered pot off the stove. She set the pot on the table with a bang and the table shook, which made her immediately remorseful. Her face turned pink in embarrassment. My father looked out the window, pretending not to see.

"So, Cynthia's teaching you to be a cowgirl," my father said to me as we sat down.

"Yep," I said.

He tried a few more questions but I didn't see any point in answering. He complimented my mother on the potatoes and filled his plate and smacked his lips.

"Try to keep your food in your mouth, Carl," she said.

"Oh, yeah. Good idea," he said and smacked some more, but she didn't laugh.

Upstairs my bedroom was still full of the heat from the day. I opened my window and pulled a cigarette out from the pack taped to the back of my dresser. On top of the dresser were pictures of my friends from Saint Cloud that I'd planned to put up; I threw the pictures in a drawer. Then I stuck the cigarette pack in my jeans pocket and headed back out the door and across the field to the creek, and then beyond the creek. At the edge of the poplar trees that bordered Auntie Katie's yard, I cupped my hand around my eyes and peered inside the house. The lights in the kitchen were on. The rest of her house was dark, except for the top left window. Cynthia was sitting at a desk, her thick hair lying down her back. I sat at the base of a poplar tree on the grass and lit up. I imagined what she was doing, writing a letter to someone, or would she keep a diary. I smoked five cigarettes, until my throat swelled up and head pounded and I felt familiar to myself again.

Just then, Cynthia leaned back in her chair and looked out the window. I stood up but I didn't step out of the trees. She moved her chair in front of the window and seemed to look right at me; she must have seen the smoke. She stood up and came closer to the window and knelt with her hands on the sill. To this day I believe she saw me there—that we were looking at each other—but it's possible she didn't see me. It's possible she was just looking into the trees like she did every other night of her life. I thought about calling up to her, trying to get her to come down and smoke with me. And finally I got so uncomfortable, I started to feel a little crazy and I turned and ran across the field and creek back home.

On the days when I worked with my father, we'd stop at Aunt Katie's house. Cynthia and I brushed Eda and Classic, while my father went in the house and talked with Aunt Katie. Her husband had died two years before. When Cynthia and I would go inside the house for a glass of water, they would be sitting at the kitchen table talking about baseball games or the weather or sometimes arguing about politics. Katie did most of the talking. My father's red cap would sit on the table and one leg would be on a chair— comfortable the way he hadn't looked at our house for a while. Aunt Katie would be leaning forward holding her coffee cup in both hands. They didn't pay much attention to us, except Aunt Katie would say "Don't get into trouble." And once, when my dad was in the bathroom, she looked right at me and said, "None of this" and put her two fingers up to her mouth like she had a cigarette.

My father didn't talk a lot about his youth, but I knew that before he'd married my mother he had dated Auntie Katie—that's how my mother and father met—and there was some story about the way they broke up. My brothers told me they had once found a picture in Dad's business closet of my dad and Katie sitting on top of a Buick kissing.

One afternoon when we were testing cows I asked him. "Why did you marry Mom and not Katie?"

"I married the woman I loved," he said. "Besides, your mother talked less."

"No, really, were you in love with Katie?"

My father handed me the thermometer and started washing his boots. His face was serious, thoughtful. "Not love," he said. "But something else."

At the corner of our barn was my favorite chicken, favorite because it had a lopsided body and a patch of feathers missing on one side as if someone had plucked them, and because it followed me around when I was setting out my bones behind the house. Early on I had dressed the chicken in an old doll shirt, and tatters of the pink collar still hung around its neck, just the sort of thing Cynthia would hate, but for some reason I didn't understand that.

"Cluck, cluck," I said, and petted the chicken. I squatted to look into the chicken's red eyes. "I love you," I said. The chicken jerked its head. "More than anything," I said. I picked it up and started walking toward the field; I had a vague notion that I would give the chicken to Cynthia, and that she would cure it. Or maybe I just wanted to show her how much the chicken loved me. At the bottom of the hill a toad scrambled under my foot and I took it to mean I was on my way to the right thing. The chicken pulsed under my arm but didn't put up a fuss—another sign.

I stood on the porch outside Cynthia's house. Between the screen and aluminum door a fly was trapped. I let the fly out. I could see into the kitchen; fabric laid out across the table, green with rose print. Aunt Katie came out of the back room in a big blue shirt, no pants. The shirt hung down to her knees; her legs were skinny but her knees were blubbery.

"You again," she said, picking the scissors off the table.

"Me," I said.

"How long you been here? You have a chicken for me today?"

I put the chicken on the porch and circled my fingers and thumb around my eye like a mask. "Hoo. Haa," I said.

She laughed, but it was more a laughing at. "You are a funny kid," she said. "Odd."

"Is Cynthia home yet?"

"No, she's not home. You need to get another hobby."

I sat down on the porch with my chicken. A car that looked familiar but that I hadn't noticed when I came up was in the driveway behind the shed. After a few minutes Auntie Katie opened the kitchen door, wearing pants, and yelled out, "If you're gonna sit there, Miss City Pants, why don't you work?"

"What do you want me to do?"

She pointed me toward a shovel that looked new on the porch and then toward the chicken coop.

The shed had a foot of straw and chicken poop on the floor and iron poles lying on it. I stacked the poles behind the shed and started shoveling the dirty straw into a wheelbarrow I found in the barn. The sun was coming in the door and warming my legs as I worked, and soon I could feel my sweat and then I could feel a shadow over me—someone standing in the doorway watching me. I shoveled for a while more slowly and then I went out.

She was sitting up against the coop chaining dandelions.

"I brought you a crazy chicken," I said, but she didn't answer. I sat in front of her. Something was different about her face, a bluish hue on her cheekbone.

"What happened to your face?" I asked.

"My mom."

"Why'd she hit you."

Cynthia kept chaining. "The reason don't matter," she said. "She just gets mad and swats because she can't make things how she wants."

"What does she want?"

Cynthia finished off the chain and looped it over the chicken's head, which I think now must have been a bit of a concession. "She wants love," she said, looking at me. "And someone to stay on the farm with her. My brothers want to sell."

"What would you do then? Where would you go?"

"Well, it wouldn't be for a while and I don't know. I guess I'd be married by then."

"Oh," I said. As it turned out, in five years her brothers would sell and Cynthia would marry a farmer in the area, not anyone I knew, but then the idea sounded entirely foreign to me; still I felt slightly threatened. My heart beat faster and I wiped a drop of cold sweat from my lip.

As Cynthia and I talked, I heard the low hum of a car driving out onto the road and I saw Alquin Schultz's thin face behind the wheel.

The sky was doing something funny now. The wind was starting to push the clouds together in a bunch and they gathered even more darkness, like a crowd of people coming together against the blue.

We walked to the creek. Cynthia's legs were skinny like her mother's, the backs of her knees doughy and unglamorous and I liked that. I liked looking at her. We sat down and the dampness from the morning seeped through my jeans.

"You're looking at me," she said, not in a coy or irritated way, but like she was pleased.

A piece of grass or dandelion stem stuck to her chin. Her mouth seemed like a gate to something, but it wasn't because of beauty— her lips were often red and chapped. It wasn't the outside I wanted, or at least that's how it seemed. I wanted to see down Cynthia's throat, to see the inside of Cynthia. I told her stories about my old school, and I told her how lonely I'd been there and until I said it I didn't even know it was true. Cynthia watched me attentively while I spoke, her mouth slightly open. At the time, I believed Cynthia felt the way I felt—I didn't question it. But now I can see that Cynthia had compartments inside her, a groove where she kept her secrets, a certain country girl hardheadedness and -heartedness that passed as practicality, as good sense.

For the rest of spring, when I didn't have to work with my dad, I'd show up at Cynthia's barn at eight a.m. when milking was finished. I'd help her wash the milk machine, sweep out the barn, pick rocks. Sometimes we'd bicycle up and down the road or walk the fields and gather bones, cow bones but also bones from possums or raccoons: femurs, jaws, skulls. We would haul the bones over to my house and bleach them and lay them out on the hill and lay ourselves on the grass or, when the grass was wet, borrow a blanket from my mother's closet in the basement. We lay with our heads in the shade and our bodies in the sun. Cynthia had a heavy breath. I have always been afraid to really let myself breathe—I think the sound gives me away—but Cynthia had no such self-consciousness. I could hear her lungs filling up and her breath sliding against her teeth.

"What do you like?" I asked her once.

She looked at me as if she were trying to see if I were really listening. "I like to hike around."

We fell asleep on the blanket and dreams swept in. Blackness behind the lid, white arms reaching toward me.

"What sound do you like best?" I asked her another time.

"The sound of the barn door opening in the morning. This isn't a sound but I like the smell of our kitchen drawers."

One afternoon while we were hiking, Cynthia found a circular piece of bone—maybe a piece of squirrel skull—and she slipped it onto her finger like a ring, holding her hand up to the sun and saying, "I pronounce myself Mrs. Bone." Later, when we were standing at the edge of her field under the poplars saying goodnight, I asked if I could have the ring. Leaning close and looking into my eyes, Cynthia took my wrist and held my hand out and slipped the bone on my finger.

I think these times with Cynthia were my first feelings of sexual desire and longing. When I wasn't with Cynthia, when she wasn't in my view or I couldn't hear her, I began to feel panicked, a fractured buzzing in my head, a restlessness in my legs. Sometimes Cynthia would stay for supper at my house and more often I'd eat at hers, and Aunt Katie started to tease me. "Better watch out," she'd say. "You're starting to look like me." A few times I slept at Cynthia's house and we'd stay up late talking and then I'd stay up later, listening to her breathe, watching her. I didn't want to touch her—probably later everyone thought I did and that's what riled them—but that wasn't the point. Consummation of desire wasn't at the center of my feelings. I was happy to feel her near me, to sit next to her at the kitchen table and cut fabric for her mother, or to pick rocks behind the cart and tractor her brother drove, and, occasionally, to sit next to her while she drove the tractor.

My mother stood on a chair throwing coats and belts and gloves out of a hall closet. My father sat in the living room.

"Where are you going?" she asked.

"Out, out," I said.

"Out out to Cynthia's out," she said. "You've been out all day with Cynthia; why don't you help me sort this stuff?"

"I'm meeting Cynthia at the creek—I'll sort tomorrow."

She threw out a hat, which had been mine in third grade, a dirty white fur hood with fur balls on the ties that kids and some silly adults wore in the late sixties. I picked it up and put it on—the hat was too small; it perched on my head, the balls swinging.

"Your head used to drown in that thing," my mother said, looking down at me from her chair. All spring, since we'd moved, she'd had a worried look about her, her eyebrows furrowed, her forehead creased. She had been distracted and I had been going around as if I were invisible, which suited me. But now she was looking at me and her forehead was smooth, but sad, or maybe disappointed; I couldn't say exactly with what.

My father walked through to the kitchen. "You're not going out," he said, and I could tell they had talked about it. "And you're coming with me tomorrow."

I took off the hat.

"Your Aunt Katie doesn't have to feed you every night," my mother said.

"She doesn't mind," I said.

"Of course she doesn't mind," my mother said. "But it's no good to push a good thing. And there are other kids around too," she added in a weak voice.

"Okay. Okay." I said, and batted the fur balls to make her smile, but inside me something choked. I felt as if my mind had been thrown against my forehead. My mouth became dry. I helped my mother sort through the stuff on the floor and went to bed.

That night I lay awake and felt a wheel turning in me. Cynthia's face was in front of me, her wide, blue-green eyes and then her white arms. I could feel this longing, but it wasn't soft the way it had been. It pulled at me. I got up and went downstairs. My father had fallen asleep in a chair in the living room, like a guard at the foot of the stairs. His shoes lay on the floor under his footstool. I hadn't really looked at him for a long time, it seemed. I didn't even know if he liked living here, liked his new job, though he seemed happy enough. His head lay to one side and his jaw hung slightly open; he had a lopsided face that scared me. Later, when he had a series of small strokes and the left side of his face slackened, making him look dopey, less harsh, less the centurion, I would remember how he had looked that night.

I put my hand out and touched the bagged-up part of his sock. I couldn't understand that I would pass through this new internal state. The panic took me over, like a flu. I stepped through the kitchen and stood on the steps outside the house, looking toward Cynthia's house, wondering if the light was on in her bedroom. I tiptoed into the kitchen and picked up the phone quietly.

"Who is this?" Auntie Katie's groggy voice.

I hung up, but even in that moment I felt closer—through the phone line I could feel the air and smells in Cynthia's house, hear her footsteps going up her stairs.

When I turned around my father was standing in the kitchen door, rubbing his eyes with the heels of his hand. He had been watching me. I am trying to see the look on his face now. Embarrassed, confused. And I think I saw pity.

My brothers arrived a week before the town's summer festival, which included a parade and a German accordion band and polka dance. My parents decided we would, as a family, help build the platform for the dance on Main Street, along with ten people from town and a few neighbors. Alquin Schultz worked beside me, looking thinner and more miserable than he had when I'd seen him talking to the cow. We hammered and sawed and sanded wood. When we got home I was put to work in the house helping my mother clean or cook or put up shelves. The house had filled with boxes and my brothers' noise, running in and out for food and water. They set up tents in the yard and when they weren't working they threw footballs and basketballs and softballs to each other. They teased me about my skulls and my cigarettes—"Nora we adora but your breath's a horra"—and they especially teased me about my overalls that Cynthia had given me and which I wore everywhere now.

During the day I was distracted enough, but every night I sneaked down the stairs and called Cynthia's house. If Auntie Katie answered, sometimes I'd hang up. Often Cynthia would answer and we'd talk about anything, Classic and Eda, what we did that day, what we ate. Once I asked, "Do you miss me?" and she laughed.

Sometimes I'd sit in the corner of our kitchen and hold on to the phone after she'd hung up, listening to the silence. We had made plans to meet at the dance on Sunday and that week I was waiting and in the waiting I began to feel I didn't exist. I did my chores, I painted the dance platform with my brothers, who watched me out of the corners of their eyes, and I fed and groomed the six-month heifer my father bought me from Aunt Katie's that I named Eda Two. But all through it I thought of Cynthia's breath and the sound of her voice. In the middle of the night I'd get up and pace the hallways and then stand on our porch looking into the blackness toward her house.

The waiting was like an aura around me. An intensity. In the kitchen my mother had pinned light, happy sayings on the refrigerator that irritated me: "Smile and the World Smiles Back." "His Love Will Save You."

Two nights before the dance, I stepped into the backyard and hauled a bucket of grain from my father's shed to the trough my brothers had built for Eda Two. The air cooled and I combed the cow's bristly hair. I clipped off the dirty long sections so the new hair could grow in clean and shiny, the way Cynthia had taught me. I ran the flat of my hand down the groove in the top of her white head to the cool soggy black nose. "Smile and the world smiles back," I whispered into her groove. "Love will save me," I said.

The dance stand was like a fifty-foot gold raft floating in the middle of Main Street. Cynthia was already dancing with Auntie Katie and when she saw me she ran over and grabbed my hand, and then she pressed her sweaty forehead and nose into mine.

I had dressed in my new baby-blue hip huggers and white shirt. I had combed my hair for an hour. Cynthia was wearing blue jeans and a blouse Auntie Katie had sewn from the rose and green print fabric. The colors set off her gold hair and blue-green eyes; her cheeks were blotchy and rosy, so rosy I now think she may have been drinking.

"Follow me," she said, and she pulled me to the middle of the dance floor. "Alls you do is this, watch. One, two, three, hop. One, two, three, hop."

I stumbled through the first few dances, but then I felt the rhythm in my legs and feet. Only about ten other people were dancing and we whirled around the floor in big circles, stomping our feet on the wooden platform, the polka band blaring.

"I love this," I shouted into Cynthia's ear and she laughed.

More people must have arrived slowly, because I remember bumping into people. I remember bumping into Auntie Katie dancing with Alquin Schultz, and my mother and father. I remember whirling off, whirling and whirling with the pressure of Cynthia's hand in the middle of my back and Cynthia's breath against my temple. I could feel the squirrel-bone ring against my thigh in my pocket—I had my plans. The sky, which had started out dusky blue, deepened in color and the evening air chilled and in the growing darkness and cold I began to feel an elation. The shapes of things started to soften and now the sky and the chickens and cow skulls and creek were inside me. I slipped my hand up Cynthia's back between her shoulder blades and she looked into my eyes and I saw our future; Cynthia and I living together like man and wife. I didn't know what that meant exactly, but I married Cynthia with every feeling in me, with every sound I had heard in my fourteen years, with every breath and eyelash, with everything I knew. I married Cynthia Hinnencamp under that darkening sky, with the Melrose band thumping, the smell of sweat and corncobs and mowed church grass in the air. I married her I married her I married her.

I must have dropped to my knees. I must have dropped and folded my hands, like a declaration. I got the ring out of my pocket and took Cynthia's hand.

And, at first, they must have thought something was wrong, that I was ill or had hurt my ankle. The people around us stopped dancing, and then people around them stopped and on and on until a hush formed and the band stopped playing and I was on my knees looking up at Cynthia and I couldn't get up. Someone shifted on the wood. Someone coughed. A crow cawed.

I must have said her name out loud. I must have said something like, Cynthia, will you marry me. There was blackness at the sides of my eyes and Cynthia's wide face above me. I was on my knees looking up at her, holding her hand and trying to put the ring on it but my hands were shaking. Her mouth was open and I could see the edges of her white teeth and a sheen of sweat on her forehead and above her lip that glistened in the light. I have replayed that moment over and over across the years and still I can't see the expression on her face. At the time I thought it was love, but it could have been something else: shock, or fear, or denial. Cynthia looked down at me steadily. The twilight behind her like a frame, a deepening blue.

My father pulled me up. For a while, when I was older and telling the story, I would say it was one of my brothers, but it was my father. And Auntie Katie was standing behind him. He pulled me up by the shoulders and took my arm and dragged me off the golden platform. He walked me down the steps, past my brothers who looked away, past Alquin Schultz who looked right at me for the first time, as if he had just discovered I existed and his curiosity pulled him out of his misery for just a moment, past a line of people waiting to buy beer. As I moved past people a quiet rushed in. They must have thought something had happened from the look on my father's face and my face; they must have thought I was hurt and being taken home. And so they did what anyone would do. They stared at me.

My father's truck was parked two blocks off Main Street behind the Red Owl. He opened the passenger door and I got in. Then he stood outside before getting in himself. We sat in the dark for a few minutes, or maybe an hour. I imagine he was trying to make sense of it, maybe feeling like he did when he discovered an infected cow in a herd: "You've got to nip it in the bud," he'd say.

Finally my father cleared his throat and started the engine.

Sometimes I dream about fields full of dead cows. I dream someone is crying. I wake up and my face is smothered in the pillow, or I'll have one hand pressed against my heart.

A few times after the dance I called Cynthia in the middle of the night. One time my aunt answered. "Is this you? Listen, honey, you have to stop this. It's too late to call and we all get up early."

"I just want to talk to her," I said.

There was a long silence and my aunt sighed.

"She doesn't want to talk to you, Nora. She doesn't want to be

Heavier Than Air

friends right now, but you go on and make other friends. You just go on."

I didn't believe her. Then one night I made a plan. I stayed up looking at a map and thinking out how we would leave on the Greyhound bus that stopped at the Melrose cafe. We would first travel to Minneapolis. We would rent a room and get jobs at restaurants. I had saved my money from working with my father. I pictured Cynthia and me with our suitcases, sitting close together in the vinyl seats, drawing hearts in the dust on the windows, holding hands and talking and talking.

Before the sun came up I was crossing the creek to Cynthia's house—I didn't know exactly what I was going to do.

She was standing in the doorway of the barn, her long hair twisted over her shoulder. I hid behind the chicken coop and willed her to turn her head and look at me. I believed I could will her; I was that full of my own power. She stepped onto the gravel and I could hear the light crunches of the dry dirt and grass beneath her feet.

About ten feet from the chicken coop she jerked her head up and saw me. I had frightened her. She looked at the front door of the house and at the window where I imagined Aunt Katie stood watching her, her hands wrapped in a towel or deep in dishwater.

"Tell her you have to loose a chicken from the fence," I whispered.

She shook her head no.

"It's okay," I said. "I have a plan."

She shook her head no.

She spoke into the collar of her coat and I could barely hear her. "Go away," she said.

"You don't mean that, Cynthia. Katie told you you had to say that."

"Kate hasn't told me anything."

"Then my father," I said.

She shook her head no and her long hair fell loose over her

shoulders. "It was a mistake," she said. "It was a stupid thing to do."

I pressed my cheek to the wood of the chicken house. Cynthia turned her head toward me then, and pulled her hair away from her face. She was showing me her face full, so I could see there were no bruises or red marks—Katie hadn't hit her; Katie hadn't told her what to say. She showed me her face so I could see it was her talking, Cynthia talking, saying what she wanted.

"I don't want you near me," she said. "Go home."

In the hottest part of summer the corn takes on sharp edges, and thistles grow between the stalks though they can be avoided if you stay in the rows. I ran barefoot in my shorts straight at the cornstalks, smashing against the cobs, scraping the thistles against my skin. A sharp pain shot up my side and rose to my heart and I honestly believed I was having a heart attack, that my heart was cracking like an egg that falls out of a tree.

I ran but I had no idea where I was going. I couldn't smell the creek or find my regular trail. Finally, I lay down on my back in the corn and breathed shallowly, until my breath caught on the pain. My feet and calves were dotted with blood. Welts puffed out on my thighs.

The night before I moved back to Saint Cloud to live with friends of my parents, I stood under the bare light bulb in the bathroom and stared at my dark hair and tanned face in the mirror. It wasn't the fact that I was in love with Cynthia that bothered them most, that they couldn't accept, not really. It was that I was so forwardly in love, so passionately in love, so unabashedly in love, so presumptuously in love, so selfishly in love, so innocently in love. It made them anxious, as it would me today if someone I knew were to behave so strongly and so foolishly about another human being.

I picked up my cigarettes and headed back out our door. At the edge of trees that bordered Auntie's land, I cupped my hand around my eyes and peered inside the house one last time. The lights in the kitchen were on. The rest of the house was dark, except for the top left window. Lit up and Cynthia sitting at her desk.

The sun dropped until it was resting on the roof of Auntie's house, and then it sank. And it was dark. I could hear a groaning, not the groaning of trees settling at night, or of the land aching from the day, but groaning from within my own mind, a way of life trying to make room for me.

After a long while, Auntie Katie walked into the room and looked out the window. Maybe she saw me, sitting in a haze of cigarette smoke, or maybe she didn't. She reached up and shut the shade.

Wide Like an Eagle's Wings

MANNY STOOD on top of the weathered wooden cable spool in her yard, trying to see what Senator John F. Kennedy would see if he visited her family's farm on his campaign tour. Beyond their paint-peeled barn and aluminum tractor shed with the unhinged door was their clumpy cow pasture, littered with thistles and dry milk-weed pods wobbling in a dangerous sheet of unexpected September heat. Burning, burning. Uncomfortable, inhospitable.

Manny lifted her chin and unfocused her eyes from the particular shapes of things to let in a general view of the county's green and yellow pastures, field after field that eventually blended into a flat, pea-soup horizon.

Senator Kennedy would use the word *emerald*. Manny, secretary of the JFK campaign at Saint Theresa's Elementary, pictured his entourage of reporters with their yellow note pads pressed to their chests, pencils behind their ears, black cameras slung from their necks. She pictured the Senator on a platform in their gravel drive-way with his sister Eunice Shriver, Mrs. Jacqueline Kennedy, and

Pierre Salinger. His left hand in his back pocket, his right hand pointing beyond their pasture to the emerald horizon, Senator Kennedy would use the word *brilliant*. She put her left hand on her back pocket, lifted her chin, and pointed.

To what?

Jilly's baby doll's head stuck upright from a cow pie, its plastic crest of hair straining out of the manure. Would a four-year-old do this deliberately?

Manny looked down at her T-shirt hand-painted with JFK's face across the chest—a gift especially for the campaign staff from Sister Oliver—and her orange and green plaid shorts. It was a pathetic, laundry-day combination. The shirt was stained from strawberry milk—she had soaked it overnight but JFK's face had turned rosy like Santa Claus's. Her shorts were cutoffs from pants she'd been forced to sew last year in fifth grade home economics class. After erroneously placing the side seams up the back—how was she to know?—she had thrown the pants in the kitchen trash bin, but her mother had fished them out. Now every few steps Manny tugged the plaid fabric out of the crack of her butt. "What does it matter?" her older sister Helen had said this morning. "The eye of the nation is not upon you."

A crow with a rubber band in its mouth trotted in a circle behind her. "Caw caw caw," she called out, her voice fading into the heat. Some noise drifted out from the spruce trees behind the tractor shed—Jilly and her friends? Dogs? FBI? KGB? She pictured square-headed men in beige trench coats and suede gloves milling through the boughs, foraging in the spruce needles on the ground with the toes of their black polished shoes, furtively stepping over the rusted wheelbarrow and barbed chicken wire.

This morning Shawn had made fun of her in the barn. *Oh say can you see. By the tractor shed's light, what so proudly we haul, from the milk tank each morning.*

She heard rustling from the spruce trees, a squeaking? Maybe it was Charly, her dog, whining from the heat. Or Morty, the neighbor's dog, an ugly beige mutt that had never got hit by a car. Manny's dogs had had their heads sliced off by trains, hind legs mashed under tractor wheels—was that justice? But old ugly Morty was lying up against their house in the shade, chewing off ticks, and Charly had followed Shawn and Jesse down to the river to check on their silver death traps. Bloody Republicans.

Watch it, she thought. Sister Oliver had told her to watch her attitude toward her citizen brothers.

Manny took three deep yoga breaths through her throat. She was learning yoga from a book that had been mistakenly placed in the American history section at the school library: *Yogic Practices for Westerners*. She dropped into a warrior pose, fiercely lunging a sword into Mr. Richard Milhous Nixon's black heart. She breathed what the book called the "spirit of life," the spirit that Sister Oliver said was the "great unifier of citizens across the land." Citizens from Juneau, Alaska, to Tallahassee, Florida, were breathing in and out with Manny Hinnencamp. John F. Kennedy was breathing in and out. He was interested in oneness of all, unity, democracy. Did she really believe this? Manny stood on her toes and reached both arms to the sky, then dropped from the waist like a willow.

Posing made her feel like nations lived inside of her. She was more than herself—she was oneness, she was democracy. Manny Hinnencamp was interested in the mutability of the individual, the relationship between citizenry and human shape. Her mother, who was in the basement doing laundry with Helen, was shaped like Idaho because her hips had spread from having babies. She used to be shaped like Minnesota, like Manny whose hips shot straight down from her waist. At twelve, Manny was trunkish and flat-chested, with long legs and big feet like Mrs. Kennedy. Last Sunday she had spent one hour in front of the bathroom mirror trying to square her mouth like Mrs. Kennedy's. This was supposed to be a beautiful mouth, but on Manny it looked as crude and mawkish as a vomit mouth.

Now from the spruce erupted odd, high chirping sounds. She climbed down from the wooden spool. The grass was dry, crisp. With her toes curled she walked on the sides of her feet bowlegged across the lawn toward the shed. She hopped across the hot gravel to the fence, sat on the top rung, and swung her legs over. As she entered the spruce trees, shadows fluttered over her arms, and then the shade deepened. The hair on her forearms stood up, ruddy goose bumps springing around the hairs like villages in a forest.

About twenty feet from an open area covered with long, yellow spruce needles, Manny crouched and held her knees. Her sister Jilly and Viki Schmerlinger were kneeling on each side of Quinn Tuttle, their weird ten-year-old neighbor from across the river. Quinn had pulled off his shirt and was sitting with his arms spread wide like wings. His bare skinny chest glowed like a mushroom. "Feeding time," he said. His voice, which was usually high and airy like a girl's—not like Manny's but like other girls'—came out half squawk. Then he stretched out his arms even farther as he lay back ceremoniously, arching his neck and shutting his eyes. Jilly and Viki tucked their hands into their armpits and began flapping chaotically, short sputtery flaps close to their sides, as if their wing muscles were too tight or as if their elbows were attached to their sides by a short string.

Quinn looked like he was being sacrificed, like the girls were going to cut his throat. Jilly and Vicki pursed their mouths, chirping softer and softer, until the chirps were squeaks. They stopped flapping and put their mouths on Quinn's nipples.

What in the hell? Manny thought. She had never seen anything like this sight. She covered one eye and looked again, as if she could rearrange the picture. Quinn let out a moan and Manny looked up into the spruce tree boughs as if she could see the sound drifting out of the top branches. She looked down between her knees at the yellow needles. She picked up a needle and poked it into her forearm. What in the world would John F. Kennedy say to this?

Out of the spruce trees, over the fence, across the gravel driveway she plodded. A splinter from the fence was burning in the side of her foot. She limped down the driveway and turned onto the pasture road toward the cornfield. She plunged her foot up to her ankle into a pile of black dirt. Tucking her other leg against her thigh she tightened her buttocks and breathed in, out, posing as a cornstalk, the dirt cooling the splintered spot. The glow of Quinn's skinny pale chest grew over her mind—that's just how it seemed; it started as a normal size and then magnified until her whole mind filled with a pale flatness and two brown penny nipples.

The thought of Jilly putting her mouth there made Manny feel sick way down inside—worse than sick; it made her feel separate from society and she hated that feeling. Who in the world did things like that? Manny had never done that. But she had done other things. She had pooped under a tree and watched the dog eat it. But not since Sister Oliver had nominated her, and the sixth grade had voted her in, as secretary of the campaign, not since she was interested in developing oneness of all and being a good citizen.

Quinn did not understand that he was a member of society. He was the only student at Saint Theresa's who had refused to register to vote in the school election. On Wednesday during the campaign rally he had climbed into the auditorium rafters and in the middle of Sister Oliver's speech had swung across the stage on the gymnastic rope. Friday morning he had run through the halls shouting the pledge of allegiance backward.

Manny held her breath to listen for sounds from the human body. Nothing.

She recited the first amendment. Then she recited the second.

Something in the dirt tickled against her shin. An angle worm crawled up out of the hole, bunching like an accordion then lengthening out. It was scrawny and gray instead of swollen and pink. Her father was worried because the soil was dehydrated and suffering from malnutrition this year. Droopy crops. The cows were giving less milk and the family was eating game and potatoes, game and potatoes. Instead of buying her a winter coat her mother was sewing Manny a midi-coat with gold buttons. Manny tried to feel compassion for the worm—the yoga book had said all beings mattered—but it was so hard to believe that worms mattered.

Jilly stood in front of her on the pasture road in her thigh-length blue and white checkered muumuu, sewn by their mother, with the navy blue ribbon trimming the short puffed sleeves and neckline. She stood as if her neck were too weak to hold her head up, embarrassing and pathetic. Now she was staring at Manny with that cow face, probably because Quinn had gone down to the river and now Jilly wanted Manny to take her down to the river like she usually did on Sundays when they had nothing else to do.

"Don't look so innocent," Manny said. "Did your playmate go back home?"

Her sister stared, the hem of her muumuu caught in the elastic band of her panties. "Let's go to the river, Manny."

"Did you take your panties down?"

She shook her head.

"Good. Don't ever take your panties down." There, she had given her some advice. "What were you doing in the trees?"

"We were baby eagles."

"Oh, God. Listen. Eagles don't do what you were doing. They fly off cliffs and feed worms and insects to their babies. Eagles are the national symbol, don't denigrate them."

Jilly shrugged—who did she get that from? Jesse? Shawn? She hopped on one foot and then the other and then she dropped to the grassy spot and rifled through the grass for four-leaf clovers. In their bedroom Jilly had a Children's Bible full of pressed four-leaf clovers, or of three-leaf clovers with a fourth leaf taped on; they were always showing up in between their bed covers, in the underwear drawer, in Manny's social studies book. Most recently she had found a homemade four-leaf clover in her scrapbook on JFK and in her secretary notebook of the minutes to the campaign meetings.

"Luck, luck, luck. You only care about being lucky." Manny put her left hand on her back pocket and pointed at Jilly. "Today is different, you know. No, you don't. You are lucky to be a citizen of the United States." She didn't know what she was saying. Her mother had said she was speaking garbage; her father said she was spinning around with crap in her pants. Somebody else's words were in her mouth and when they came out a great distance grew between the inside of herself and the outside. Manny the secretary of the JFK campaign, Manny the member of a nation. She took a deep yoga breath, but the nation had slipped out of her: she couldn't see a nation, she couldn't smell a nation, she couldn't hear a nation. What was a nation?

"Come on," she said to Jilly. "Let's go down to the river."

Weaving through droopy cornstalks the height of Manny's head, Jilly padded along behind her in her bare feet, touching the tassels as she went by, humming in her flat, toneless pitch like someone who had never heard a bird in her life. Manny had asked her to stop singing three times but Jilly continued.

"Jilly, your song is a dirge."

"No," she said. "You are." She hummed on.

Manny suddenly felt listless and causeless and despairing, a feeling she had not experienced since the campaign began two weeks ago. But now here it was again, the day before the school vote, filling up her heart, making her legs and arms droop like the corn. JFK would lose tomorrow. Who cared anyway? Only a class. Not the real election. Not the nation. They were nothing. The President was nothing. Nothing mattered.

Where the cornfield met the top of the riverbank she stopped and yanked a cob from its stalk. She knelt and drew a square face in the dirt with a lock of hair on the forehead and an arrow nose. "That's him," she said, and handed the cob to her sister. "You draw something. Draw a flag."

"I don't want to."

"Why not? Don't you have hope?"

"Don't want it."

"Sure you do. Go ahead. Draw a four-leaf clover."

Jilly took the cob and shucked it. She picked off a hard kernel and pressed the kernel into her cheek. "Quinn flew to the river, Manny."

Putting her hands on Jilly's shoulders, Manny looked seriously into her face. Jilly had golden eyebrows and eyelashes like hers.

"Listen," Manny sighed. "You're only four. Quinn is ten. Don't do the eagle game with him anymore. The President wouldn't like it." She pointed to her T-shirt.

Jilly poked the kernel deeper into her cheek and shrugged, pulling on the loose elastic leg holes of her panties.

"I'll tell you how to be good. Imagine that you are running for the presidency and that the whole country is watching you on television. The press report on everything you do. They've got binoculars aimed right at you and every citizen of the United States depends on you. Imagine that all of your actions are for the good of the country. That may help."

Her sister stuck her tongue up behind her top lip. She looked like a baby baboon.

Manny stood up. She felt better, her faith partly restored. Sometimes it was hard for Manny to remember that Jilly needed a citizen role model.

She could see the river, a long blue snake crawling across the land, dividing it into two parts. Manny's family's side of the river, which was also Klapuke's and Schmerlinger's side, sloped and was lined with trees and shrubs; on the other side ran a narrow strip of yellow marsh like a dingy yellow ribbon. Beyond the marsh, just inside the barbed wire fence, stood Tuttle's three cows, broiling under the sun in a black and white clump.

Manny saw her two younger brothers hiking toward them up the riverbank carrying game. Trotting behind them obediently with a grouse in his mouth was Manny's dog, his fur underneath matted with mud. Shawn, who was in fifth grade, a grade behind Manny but the same size, was carrying two dead squirrels by the tail. Jesse, in second grade but still shedding baby fat, had a dead fox slung face-first over his shoulder. Blood from the corner of the fox's mouth dripped onto the chest of his white T-shirt like a fatal wound. They stopped in front of Manny.

"Dead squirrel, dead grouse, dead fox, dead everything," Shawn said, stepping toward her and shaking the squirrels in her face. Jesse mimicked by shaking the empty fox trap.

Manny's face went red. She straightened and tried to look like the secretary of a campaign.

"Our future President is speaking on TV after supper," she said to Shawn in her official voice. "It's not too late for us to stick together. The school rule said you could change party affiliations up to ten tomorrow morning."

"We don't care what he says. You're hysterical. He's not speaking to us, he's just speaking to a camera. You're hung up and weird for your age."

"He's speaking to the nation."

"But not you, you're not the nation. You're just secretary of a stupid committee. You don't love your country. If he calls a war with Russia, you'll just stay home and pinch in your butt and breathe like a nut, like you're already shot through the throat." He rolled his head and made his breath go in and out rasping absurdly like a dying person. Spittle flew off his lips onto the squirrels. Jesse rolled his head like Shawn's, fox blood spreading into his armpit. She reminded herself that they were fellow citizens and that she loved them and that made her feel good about herself. She felt full of love and bighearted—that's what one commentator had said about JFK. He had a heart big enough for the Negroes and the working people and the farmers.

"I love you," she said to her brothers. Shawn looked like he was going to choke, like his body was crawling with words he couldn't get out. He held one of the squirrels out in front of him and squeezed its smashed neck. The squirrel's pink tongue pushed out over its teeth.

"You," Shawn said, "have nothing for your country. You can't even sew."

"I will sew when I'm older," she said.

"What, like that?" He snorted at her shorts which had bunched up at the top of her thighs, the zipper lying crooked up to her waist. Manny tugged them down.

Jilly was leaning against Jesse's back pulling the fox's tail, brushing her fingers through the fur as if it were doll hair. "Pretty fox. Are you hungry? Do you want an acorn?" She held an imaginary acorn to the fox's mouth.

"Jilly, stop that. That bloody animal used to run free through the woods and wasn't harming anyone. How would you like to have your neck caught in a trap?"

Jilly laid her cheek against the fox tail and then turned around and started trudging down the bank toward the river ahead of Manny, arching her back and letting her head drop back so Manny could see her eyes and forehead upside down.

Snake River was flat and green and calm. No one was fishing in Schmerlinger's boat. Manny and Jilly walked along a path going up the river toward Klapuke's farm and the sand pile that had been by the river since Manny could remember—who knows how it got there. A mile north the river was only ten feet wide and showed its muddy bottom, but at Schmerlinger's it ballooned out to thirty feet and became deep and dark, with strong currents along the banks. Jesse, Shawn, and the Tuttle boys swam in this part of the river. A few people from town liked to troll here for pikes and crappies. Manny had fished in Schmerlinger's boat with her father, and sometimes she took Jilly out in the boat, but she never swam in the river, only in lakes. Cows pooped and peed in the river; giant snapping turtles crawled up from the bottom; bloated carp and muskrats washed up on shore.

At the sand pile ten feet up the riverbank Gary and Julie Klapuke were filling a wheelbarrow with sand. Gary and Julie were twins in Manny's grade. Gary was shoveling dirt from the bottom of the pile into the wheelbarrow that Julie was holding steady. Manny stopped to watch them. She liked the rhythm of the shovel plunging into the sand, swinging through the air, then sand spilling off into the metal barrow. Industrious. The hole in the sand pile got bigger as the barrow filled.

"What are you doing?"

"We're getting sand for our sandbox in our backyard," Gary said.

"We built a box," Julie said.

How had they thought of doing that? How did they know how to build a box for the sand, how had they thought of moving the sand from the river to their backyard? Just like last Saturday, Shawn and Jesse had clomped upstairs in their blue jeans, T-shirts, and boots; they had eaten two bowls of Froot Loops, made two jelly sandwiches, put them in a bag, and gone up the river to gather wood to build a fort. Had they dreamed of building a fort the night before? How did they know they could build a fort?

"Hold on," Manny said. "I'm interviewing people about John F. Kennedy, the soon-to-be President Elect. Do you have anything you want to say?"

Gary stuck the shovel in the ground and looked at her, puzzled. "You don't have a tape recorder."

She hadn't thought of taping anything; she hadn't known she was going to interview anyone until the words came out of her mouth, but now that they had she felt her allegiance to JFK return full force. She had started to think she might just be lurking around passing the time, something her mother had often accused her of, but now she saw her purpose in this moment.

"Are you Republicans or Democrats?"

"I'll vote Nixon, she'll vote JFK," Gary said.

"So, Julie, you say something about why you'll vote for him. What you hope he will do for us."

"I don't know what to say," Julie said. Her brow was creased. "I could sing a song."

"What song?"

"I don't know."

"I don't get what singing a song will do," Gary said. "I mean, I don't get what saying anything will do anyway since you don't have a tape recorder or your secretary notebook."

Manny understood what he was saying, but now that she was on to the idea she wanted to complete it. She didn't want to feel like a quitter, like with the sewing project.

"She has the right to speak out. It's the freedom of speech. We have to use our freedoms or they die."

"I know," Julie said. She dropped the barrow handles and went into the bushes, coming out a minute later carrying a branch fanning out with burgundy leaves. Facing up the slope away from the river she put one foot on a rock, tucked her loose hair behind her ears and cleared her throat. Manny could see her pink scalp through her thin blonde hair. Sweeping the branch through the air in front of her, her other hand cupped as if she were holding a bit of wind in it, Julie began to sing "He's Got the Whole World in His Hands," the song she had performed at their school talent show. Manny sat on her haunches in the grass and listened. Julie was a good singer; she had a voice that quivered in her chest on high notes as if her heart was about to burst with the meaning of the words. Snapping her fingers, swaying as Julie swayed, Manny let the song fill her heart. She pictured JFK standing on the embankment, his jaw square and serious, the perfect straight hem of his black suit jacket blowing in the wind.

Gary leaned his chin on the shovel handle. Jilly climbed into the hole they had been digging and crouched down as far as she could until her chin pressed into her knees. She rolled her head from side to side out of beat with the song, as if no one were singing at all and she were just in a hole moving her head for no reason, having nothing to do with anything else. Manny felt like shoving Jilly's head all the way into the hole; instead she focused on Julie's branch swaying.

On the last line, Julie waved the branch over the embankment and looked with watery blue eyes at her imaginary audience. Beyond the particulars into the general. Manny saw the banks filled with Democrats, Julie burning and shining and the future ahead of her on the brilliant emerald horizon.

Julie waved the branch one last grand stroke to cover everyone and then she let her voice waver off. A cow bellowed across the river.

Manny felt the spirit inside her lurch forward and she clapped until her hands stung. She felt completely unified. She was oneness again; Julie had given her that. Julie walked over and they hugged. "He's going to win," she said.

"Yes," Manny said.

Gary picked up his shovel and stood over Jilly, waiting for her to move. "Nixon isn't so bad," he said.

"It's okay," Manny told him. She was so sure in this moment.

Jilly had stretched out and now lay on her belly with her arms at her sides. Her tongue hung over her bottom lip like the squirrel's.

"Bury me," she said.

Manny walked over, stood behind her, and pulled her muumuu over her butt.

Julie took her place next to Gary holding the barrow. Gary started digging a new hole in the pile, dumping every other shovelful over Jilly.

Suddenly, a wild squawk came out from the trees at the back of the sand pile and out jumped Quinn Tuttle. He landed on top of the sand pile, his face and chest covered with the greenish black mud from the river bottom. He had smoothed the mud over himself until every inch above his pants was hidden. Now patches were drying on his back and arms into a crusty black skin, the whites of his eyes like a Negro's. How long had he been waiting up in the tree? Now he crouched on the top of the sand pile staring at them, and then he rose slowly, expanding his muddy wings above them. He rose and sank in graceful swoops, as if his body were truly being lifted by currents of air.

"Squawk," he said.

In her hole Jilly began making crawling motions with her arms and legs until she looked like a turtle trudging along in its dirt shell. Quinn squawked again, flew down the pile and disappeared into the bushes.

As soon as she saw Quinn, Manny felt her joy of the song deflating, her rib cage drooping over her belly. Jilly had crawled out of the hole and was staring into the bushes after him, her back and butt covered with sand.

"He's weird," Gary said, shoveling sand and dumping it into the wheelbarrow. Julie picked up the handles and braced the barrow against her hip.

"Our first load of sand," she said.

"How many loads do you have to make?"

"Seven," Gary said.

He took hold of one of the handles and they began pushing the wheelbarrow up the hill. Manny caught up to Jilly, who had headed in the direction of Quinn. She brushed her off and turned her around and they started walking in the opposite direction on the path they'd come from along the flat, green river.

Today was not the same as other days; Manny could feel it in the air. Today things mattered—maybe from now on things would matter more. Tonight JFK would speak to them in their living room because they were part of the great human race, part of the great northern plains: her brothers, her mother and Helen, Jilly, her father and her. After clearing up the supper dishes they would sit in their living room and listen to the next President speak. Her father was doing chores early so he could get in the house and shower in time to hear him. This was the first Catholic presidential candidate; Manny had thought they were all Catholic, but now she knew the lot of them were Protestants, and Nixon was a Quaker. But tonight JFK would be speaking to the citizens inside all of them. And tomorrow the Church Grove Elementary would vote, and Manny and the secretary from the Nixon campaign would sit at one of the long tables in the school cafeteria during sixth-hour study hall, with Sister Oliver monitoring them, and count the votes.

She only wished she could vote for him in the real election in November. She had already voted for him in their school poll; in fact, she had snuck into the fifth-grader line from the back door of the gymnasium so she could be polled twice. But it hadn't helped. Richard M. Nixon had been the favorite. Half of the students polled had never read the constitution. They didn't understand Sister Oliver's speech about how everything depended on each person as a member of the nation, how everything depended on seeing beyond the particulars to the horizon.

It was right when Sister Oliver had said "horizon," with both her hands on her heart, that Quinn Tuttle had come swooping down in front of the podium, staring at the seated row of campaign officials as if he were just passing the time, as if they had expected him. As he swung back toward the podium from the other direction Sister Oliver caught him in her arms and he didn't resist when she gently handed him over to Sister Madeliva. She returned to the podium, but the audience had been lost in a chaos of laughing and whispering. Sister Madeliva escorted Quinn out of the auditorium and then the fourth, fifth, and sixth graders started to line up to vote for Nixon in the poll.

The people didn't understand democracy. They didn't understand social responsibility, they didn't understand oneness—Manny herself was only just struggling to understand her rights as an individual balanced against the greater social good. She was only beginning to hope that Sister Oliver was right, that what she did really mattered.

Jilly was walking ahead of Manny on the path, humming "he's got the whole world in his hands" off-tune. Why did she like to sing so much when she couldn't hear notes? And she drew picture after picture though she couldn't draw, and just pretty much went about doing whatever she wanted with no one paying much attention, no one teaching her how to behave in a civilized manner, except their mother who sometimes told her to chew with her mouth shut. Jilly didn't seem to care about anything yet; was this normal human development? Look at her now, trudging along the path ahead of Manny, humming off-tune and not even knowing it, picking her nose and wiping it on her leg.

Last week during supper Jilly had taken the chopped-up hamburger from her plate with her fingers and stuffed it into the vents of the radiator behind her chair! By nighttime the weather had grown unusually chilly, so their father put the heat on low and in the middle of the night the smell of burned hamburger filled their bedrooms, waking them up. When her father unscrewed the cover from the radiator he found hamburger sizzling in all the coils from the floorboard up to the vents, a summer's worth of Jilly's cruddy dried-up hamburger that looked like rabbit turds.

Jilly was carrying a rock shaped like an arrowhead. Four-leaf clovers and rocks shaped like arrowheads were her specialty. She was poking the point of the rock into her ear; this was also her specialty, stuffing things into her ears or into her nose, like the day after Christmas when they had to rush her to the hospital with her eyes rolled into her head and her back arched. Jilly had ridden in the back seat with Manny, draped over Manny's lap with her mouth wide open, the whites of her eyes staring blank as a page at Manny as if to say *don't worry, nothing matters, I am no one, you are no one.*

When they got to the hospital the surgeon emptied two corn kernels and four red Mexican jumping beans from Jilly's sinus passages. Why in the world would she stuff all that up her nose? Manny had never stuffed things up her nose. Had John F. Kennedy or Jacqueline or Ethel Kennedy, or Pierre Salinger, or Sargent Shriver ever stuffed things up their noses? Sometimes it was hard for her to tell if her family and the people she knew were normal American citizens or if they were out of sync.

"Jilly, I'm so tired of telling you things. I don't even think you hear me. Do you hear me? Am I really here?"

"No," Jilly said, pointing her arrowhead into the sky.

Manny wished the Senator would mention their names—she knew he wouldn't, of course he wouldn't because he didn't even know them personally. But to hear their names spoken, to hear her family's names stretching out of his mouth: "Manny, Jilly, Helen, Mr. and Mrs. Hinnencamp, and the boys, I want to tell you that you are part of America. You are what makes this country the grand nation that it is. We need you and your vote in the upcoming election. We the people of this country must unite and must not fear."

The first time he had spoken as a presidential candidate on television had taken them by surprise. Manny had put the dishes into the cupboards and was wandering around the edges of the living room, watching her family wait for their Disney program through the crack in the divider her mother had put up to stop kids from gawking at their TV. Helen was sitting in a chair in her slip; she had just come home from town and was hemming up her waitress uniform. Shawn and Jesse were playing Crazy Eights on the floor, Shawn sipping Kool-Aid out of their green plastic pitcher, no one telling him to use a cup. Her mother sat in the recliner with a piece of rhubarb kugel on her lap, a slice of Velveeta draped over the top of the kugel like a blanket. She had heated the kugel in the oven on low—heating desserts on low is what her mother did on Sunday nights. Her father was lying on his side on the couch with a pillow under his neck, asleep.

And suddenly John F. Kennedy appeared, sitting behind a dark wooden desk, his hands folded, resting on a notepad.

"My fellow Americans," he said.

Up ahead about fifty feet, just before the river narrowed, was Schmerlinger's metal rowboat. She had daydreamed them all the way to Schmerlingers! Manny had the idea that they could get into the boat and row back down the river where they'd started from. It seemed like such a long way back, just going along the river path, stepping over rocks and ducking under branches. The sun was dropping and changing the color of things, making the water look darker, deeper. The heat was turning to coolness. The horizon looked gray.

When they reached the boat Manny started pushing it off shore into the water. "Come on," she said. "Let's get into the boat."

Jilly looked at the boat. "I don't want to get into the boat."

"We'll go back down the river and then go home and watch the President."

"I don't want to."

Manny straightened up and sighed. She put one foot on the boat and rocked it, listening to the water lap against the metal. "Why? I mean, do you have a reason, because if you have a reason we can discuss it."

Manny herself knew there was a reason—Schmerlinger's rule was they had to leave the boat where they found it and they had to wear life jackets. Jilly had never gone in the boat without a life jacket, and normally Manny wouldn't either, but her legs were tired and she kept thinking how they could just row down the river back to where Julie and Gary were hauling sand and maybe Julie would sing another song and then Manny and Jilly would walk a short ways instead of a long ways home.

Manny pushed the boat with her foot and stared at Jilly. "Well, I'm waiting," she said.

"I can't swim."

"Yes you can. Remember the dog paddle?" Last Sunday the family had had a picnic at Lake Sylvia and Manny had spent the day teaching Jilly the dog paddle. She paddled back and forth close to shore to demonstrate and then she carried Jilly into the water and held her afloat while Jilly paddled and kicked. The first times Manny let go Jilly sank, but the third time Jilly had paddled a few feet, and the fourth time a few feet more. By sunset, Jilly could paddle from the shore to Manny's chest. "Jilly the citizen fish! Jilly the citizen sea monster!" Manny had cheered, scooping her up and holding her over her head.

Now at the river Jilly stared back at Manny, then trudged forward and put her hands in the air for Manny to pick her up. She was so light—it always took Manny by surprise how her hands could fit around Jilly's rib cage and lift her off the ground, and how Jilly would let her do this, let her body be lifted up and put places.

Jilly sat in the middle of the front bench, her hands folded in her lap, her dirty feet hanging over the floor of the boat, heels bumping against the metal side of the seat.

"What happened to your rock?"

"I dropped it." She pointed to shore.

"You could have brought the rock in the boat. There's no law against it."

Manny climbed into the boat and with an oar pushed them off into the river.

The air was cool on the river, the water slow. Breathing through her throat she rowed with the sluggish current, listening to the oars dip into the water, swing forward with a creak, dip and swing, the water gliding around them, carrying them. Drips of water landed on her knees.

A fishing boat was puttering toward them. As it approached, Manny saw Martha Tool, a ninth grader, in her straw fishing hat and two-piece black bathing suit. Martha slowed her boat.

"What did you catch?" Manny asked.

"Ten crappie." A pack of cigarettes dangled from her neck on a white shoe lace. She fished out a cigarette and lit it and blew out smoke from under her hat.

"Who are you going to vote for?" Manny asked.

"What?" She was already puttering past. The waves from her boat rolled their boat.

"In the high school election," Manny yelled. "Who will you vote for?"

Martha took a drag and shook her head.

Manny stood up in the boat and pointed to her T-shirt.

Martha smiled and waved her cigarette and held up her ten crappies.

John F. Kennedy liked boats; he and Jacqueline and their children went yachting on the Atlantic Ocean in beige pants and white button-down shirts—she had seen a picture of them in the *Times* at the library—JFK at the wheel of a yacht looking over the ocean, the water parting ahead of him, the wind blowing one end of his collar onto his neck. Jacqueline was sitting on the bench next to him with one hand braced on the boat side, her square lips smiling, her big

Heavier Than Air

feet in white shoes with a navy blue strip around the sole. This is what he did for relaxation, this is what he did to hold himself up through the storm of politics, as Pierre Salinger had said in the article.

The rowing motion was making the fabric of her shorts rub against the skin in her crack. Chafing, her mother would say, but it felt more like sawing, and she could feel a rash burning on her inner thighs and deep up in her butt. She pulled the shorts out, then rowed, pulled them out, then rowed. These particulars were the things that could drive a person crazy. She counted her breaths and looked over Jilly's head down the long blue river that connected them to the Mississippi, which ran down the map to the Gulf of Mexico and the Atlantic Ocean. She tried to rise above the nonsense. What did chafing have to do with oneness, with the fate of the nation, with how JFK was going to lift them up into a larger place?

Before that Sunday night, Manny had never seen a presidential candidate. She felt a tingling up her back, her heart pounding. Shawn held the pitcher of Kool-Aid up to his mouth but he wasn't drinking; he was frozen listening to the man on the TV screen. The man had a square head and square jaw and wavy brown hair—he looked a little bit like her father or one of her uncles and when her mother commented on this her father sat up and said, "By god, he could almost be my brother Patrick." John Kennedy was looking into their living room with his dark eyes; he was holding her gaze, he wasn't blinking, he was speaking to them, his words stretching out of his mouth in an accent she had never heard before, as if someone were pulling the sides of his mouth wide, as if his words were being stretched to cover the whole country. Manny hooked the white elastic straps of her pajama bottoms under her feet and stretched the pants way up to her chest. She could almost see Mr. Kennedy's words coming out of the television and filling their living room. He was the one who was going to change their lives, the one who would make things different. He was the one who would make Manny's existence count.

On the marsh side of the river up ahead was the Tuttles' big oak. As Manny approached she could see muddy feet hanging out of the branches.

She stopped rowing about ten feet before the tree. A wind rushed up the river through the branches making the leaves flutter and part and for a moment she could see Quinn standing on a branch totally naked, his chest spotted with mud, his arms spread wide, wide like an eagle's wings. She saw Jilly look up and walk to the side of the boat; Jilly tucked her hands under her arms and opened and closed her mouth, silently chirping. And as Manny began to leave her seat, she saw Jilly bump against the side of the boat and tip into the water with a splash. Drops landed on Manny's face.

Jilly was in the river.

Jilly was splashing her hands and looking up at Manny. Jilly was splashing her hands and looking up at Manny and gulping water.

"Jilly," Manny shouted. "Do your dog paddle!"

Why wasn't she paddling? She was only a few feet from the boat, why didn't she swim? Manny called again and then she showed her, to remind her. She stretched her neck out and paddled through the air. But Jilly kept splashing her hands like someone who had never swum in her life.

Manny grasped the oar by the tip of the handle and stretched over the side of the boat, but Jilly couldn't lift her hands out of the water. And now the current was pulling her away and the oar slipped out of Manny's grasp.

"Help!" Manny shouted. "Quinn! Get help!"

Jilly was going down. She was looking up at Manny going down. Her face shimmering in the water, shimmering just under the water. Bubbles were coming out of her mouth and Manny could see

Heavier Than Air

her pushing her teeth to the surface of the water, her two overly large front teeth aimed for the sky, breaking the water that fit like a glove around her face.

As if someone had tugged her from below, Jilly dropped under.

Manny took a deep breath and dove into the water. She was a terrific swimmer, but the river frightened her. She could feel the steady tug of the current. Her ears stopped with cold and her heart thudded in her chest. About three feet under the surface Jilly was waving her arms, her muumuu tangled under her armpits, the dark blue trim flapping as Jilly flapped. She looked like she was climbing, her pale legs moving ghostly in the murky river water. Manny swam through the cold to Jilly. As she reached out for her arm, Jilly struck out with her other arm hitting Manny in the eye. She grabbed onto Manny's T-shirt and climbed up and clung to Manny's neck and now they were both going down. Manny kicked for the surface but her body was going down. It was going to be like this—she thought clearly, and it seemed so impossible, so startling and frightening and ridiculous. She looked up through the particles floating in the water and saw the sun going down. She was a beautiful swimmer and John F. Kennedy was going to be President but it was going to be like this. Her lungs grew large in her chest, too large, pressing into her rib cage, the air welling up inside her and pushing against her skull. Jilly was pressing her body into Manny as if Manny were a soft bed of grass, as if she were land. Her heart beat against Manny's chest and then her body jerked and her arms loosened. Jilly looked up at Manny, her eyes rolled back, the whites looking up at Manny and saying *don't leave me, it doesn't matter, you are nothing, this is nothing.*

Manny pried Jilly's arms off her neck and kicked to the surface. She opened her mouth and air rushed inside her making her dizzy. Floating on her back, she gulped air. She knew what to do. She took a deep breath and dove back down.

The river seemed thicker now. Jilly was sinking slowly into the darker water, her muumuu wafting over her head, a gray water flower with pale tendril legs. Manny pulled the muumuu down. Jilly's mouth was already slack and open and water slipped in past her teeth. Water entered her like a cave, no difference between air and water.

Wrapping one arm around her sister's waist, Manny pulled her toward the surface.

The sky was white. The current had carried them down the river about fifty feet past the big oak where they had seen Quinn. Holding her sister afloat with one hand on her back, Manny kicked toward the Tuttles' marshy shore. She dragged Jilly through the weeds and mud and laid her gently out on her stomach and tipped her face to one side so her cheek rested on the spongy yellow grass. She knew what to do. She had seen it on TV once. Kneeling with Jilly's head between her legs, she grasped Jilly's small wrists and began pumping her arms at her sides. Up over her head and down to her hips. She flapped Jilly's arms up and down, taking deep yoga breaths, imagining her breath one with Jilly's breath. Imagining oneness.

A warm trickle of blood rolled out of her eye where Jilly had struck her and ran onto Jilly's wet hair. She felt her arms grow heavier and her eyelid sting and go numb. Blackness was settling around them, slowly, shutting out her view of anything beyond Jilly's body and her body.

Her family would be sitting in front of the television listening to the next President end his speech. Her mother would ask the boys where in the world the girls had gone and Manny's father would look out the window and wonder whether he should go out and get them. But they had stayed out late on hot nights before. Once she and Jilly had dragged their blankets from their bed and slept in the yard and no one knew it until her father came out to do chores early the next morning. But they would wonder why Manny would miss the President. "She's going to miss him," Shawn might say. Maybe they would think she had come back to her senses, that she was going to be the old Manny who didn't pose on one leg in the yard and talk about democracy. That she would just read her mysteries and sing Frank Sinatra songs like everyone else.

Manny pumped her sister's arms wide, wide like an eagle's wings. She looked up at the sky—she thought she could hear Julie's song from earlier, "he's got the whole world in his hands," and she began to hum it, softly, methodically, breathing in and out. Her lungs burned and that felt good, warm, as her skin prickled with goose bumps and a deep cold began settling into her chest.

While she worked she could see the future. She could see herself carrying Jilly around the yellow ribbonlike edge of Tuttle's land, over the small foot bridge back to where Julie and Gary had gathered the sand. She would carry her up the riverbank and through the cornfield. She would carry her sister's dead body into their house and lay her on their old snagged brown couch, where there had never been a dead body.

The river was black. The horizon was gray and murky. A blade of grass cut into Manny's thigh, a red ant crawled up her arm. All Manny could hear was her own breathing. I am breathing, she thought. It was as small as that. Breath.

La Maison de Madame Durard

HOPING IT would make her seem dramatic, like someone from out of town, Marie undid the buttons on her coat so the fabric fell open around her hips and the hem draped her ankles. Peter Schneiweiss and a few townies were bowling. At the end of the bar, in her jacket with squirrel fur around the collar, Chrissy leaned her bony hip on a stool, like some sort of time traveler from the wild west. Marie walked over and leaned her back up against the bar.

"Hey," she said, poking a finger into Chrissy's side.

"Hey," Chrissy said without moving her unlit cigarette. Her foot on the bottom rung of the stool was tapping—she was already buzzed on something.

"You ready to have some fun?" she asked.

Behind the bar, Peter's father stopped wiping glasses and leaned over to stick his face between their heads. Deep lines ran from his mouth to his eyes, which made him look sewn together like Frankenstein's monster. Marie pictured his wife in their apartment

upstairs, sitting on a sofa night after night, watching TV and waiting for him to come home after closing the bowling alley.

"You little girls want anything?" he asked. "Potato chips, Good
'n Fruity, Life Savers?"

Chrissy rolled her eyes and pushed off for the bathroom. Marie
followed.

It was dim and smelled like an overdose of air freshener and stale
urine. Marie followed Chrissy into the first stall and bolted the
door. On the back of the toilet, Chrissy set her pocket mirror, an
X-acto knife she'd stolen from seventh-hour industrial arts, and a
tiny plastic bag half full of powdered pot residue—Chrissy called
it THC. Marie's stomach gurgled from nervousness. Once she had
snorted nutmeg in Chrissy's basement, but nothing had happened,
just a slight headache. Now she remembered what the school counselor had said in his speech to the freshman class about drugs.
Once you begin you can't stop. Marie hoped she wouldn't stop; she
hoped this was the beginning of a new life for her.

Chrissy sucked the powder up her nose with a section of cafeteria
straw, looked up and smiled with watery eyes at Marie.

The restroom door squeaked open, then footsteps. Pressing her
finger against her mouth, Chrissy handed the mirror to Marie, and
climbed on the toilet tank. Marie sat in front of her on the edge of
the seat—holding the mirror and straw—and peered through the
crack between the door and frame. Mrs. Braegelman, crazy Marilyn
Braegelman's mother, ambled into the stall next to theirs and peed
like there was no tomorrow. She came out of the stall and stood
on her tiptoes in front of the mirror above the sink, tugging at her
girdle through her beige slacks and checking out her flat, wide behind. Marie looked into Mrs. Braegelman's dissatisfied eyes in the
mirror.

"Who's in there?" Mrs. Braegelman glanced across the room at
the closed stall door.

"It's just Marie Ann Schroeder," she answered. "One of Joseph Schroeder's daughters."

Mrs. Braegelman looked back in the mirror and stuck her finger under her glasses to wipe her eye. "How's your sister doing?"

Marie's older sister was on scholarship studying to become a physical therapist at the University of Wisconsin.

"She dropped out of college," Marie lied. "We think she joined a commune in California."

Chrissy dug her boot into Marie's behind.

"Really?" Mrs. Braegelman said. She shook her head and walked out the door. Chrissy let out a hiss, climbed down from the tank and left the stall.

Marie felt a little guilty, not because she'd lied but because she loved her sister and because once Mrs. Braegelman had given her a ride home from school, even though it was miles out of her way. She didn't know why she had to lie about these things. She wished her sister had joined a commune, and that she and Chrissy could go live with her. But one weekend, during Christmas break, they had gone to visit her sister at the University of Wisconsin in Madison, and all they had done was pop popcorn and watch TV in the dorm room. Chrissy fell asleep at eight p.m. "Isn't there some sort of demonstration or love-in we could go to?" Marie asked. Her sister had just laughed and poured more butter on Marie's popcorn.

Marie didn't know if she would have had the guts to go to a demonstration or a love-in. Sometimes at night she sat up in bed and counted the hours she'd already lost watching television, or driving her uncle's tractor around the field, or babysitting her brothers and sisters. Two thousand at least. One night she'd climbed on top of their shed in the backyard. Balancing on the flats of her feet, she walked back and forth across the apex of the roof and recited phrases she'd learned from her foreign language dictionaries. She gazed out over the rolling hills and pasture, pretending she was in the northern hills of France, where one of her great-great-grandmothers had been born. "Voila! La maison de Madame Durard," she said.

In the bowling alley restroom, Marie sat in the stall and looked at her face divided by the crooked line of powder on the pocket mirror. Sucking the powder deep into her nose, she felt a sharp pain shoot up her nasal passages and behind her eyes; the back of her throat tasted bitter.

"Chrissy, do you realize we're fifteen and everything important on the planet is taking place without us?"

Chrissy drank some water and blew her nose. "Life is small," she said. It was a quote from the only poem she had read for second-hour English.

Marie tried to pee. She imagined the powder absorbing into the vessels of her nose, her cells opening up.

At lane five, everything glowed and expanded: the long, shiny wooden lanes; the bright white walls; the bowling pins. Chrissy sat in the scoring chair rearranging the pencils in the cup, then the cigarettes in her pack. She switched one unlit cigarette for another.

The three men at the lane next to theirs wore green and white hats advertising Black Cat Snowmobiles and carried vinyl bowling bags. One man, the bus driver who had taken them to and from junior high last year, had a blond mustache that hid his whole top lip. He nudged the guy next to him, and they glanced at Marie and Chrissy, then rolled their eyes. Rednecks.

She flipped them a hidden double bird below the bench. She wanted to lean over the booth toward them and hiss, "I am a drug addict." She had tied her white button-down shirt above her hip huggers so a strip of skin showed. Now she bent over to take off her shoes and showed Mr. Moustache the crack of her butt.

"Your ass is showing," Chrissy said.

"I know my ass is showing," Marie said. "It's called body language."

Chrissy shook her head; she didn't get it.

Marie swung her hips as she walked over to the jukebox and pushed the buttons in for "Gypsies, Tramps and Thieves." She wished she were part Lebanese, like Cher, or a real drug addict traveling around the world like Janice Joplin: Marie with long black hair like Chrissy's instead of blond. Marie swinging her hips across the five lanes of the bowling alley, singing "Gypsies" in a throaty low voice. Applause, applause.

Peter Schneiweiss sat about two feet away from the jukebox with his face buried in a big hardcover book.

"What you reading?" Marie asked him.

Without looking at her, he held the book up in front of her face: *Communist Manifesto*, by Karl Marx. On the bottom half of the cover a comet shot out of the night—it looked as if it were going to shoot off the cover.

"How ethereal," she said. "La vie est petite."

When Marie got back to their booth, Chrissy was still bent over undoing her boots to put on her bowling shoes.

"Chrissy, we'll be old or dead before you get those off."

Chrissy looked up. The whites of her eyes were ultra white and her pupils had spread out over her iris. She held out her foot. Marie took the heel, tugged, dropped the boot on the floor.

While waiting for the pins to reset, Marie picked through the balls on their rack. It was the last bowl in the game. She weighed each one carefully and wiggled her fingers inside the holes. She settled on her usual, the black ball with blue swirls.

"That ball's too heavy for you," a loud voice came from behind her. Mr. Mustache leaned back in his chair and grinned at her. He took a swig of beer and Marie saw the lump move down his red neck and under his plaid shirt collar. She felt like saying "get a lip."

"What do you mean?" she said.

"Well, you go in the gutter with it every time."

"I just got five down," she said.

"You did?" He bugged his eyes down her lane and then back at Chrissy and her. "Why, looked like just another gutter ball to me."

Marie stepped up to the blue line. The ten pin stands for all the rednecks in this town. The next for everyone who thinks they're smarter than me, the next for Mr. Hegle for calling me a goddamn pig for eating my sandwich in world geography. She closed her eyes and tried to think bigger than just herself. Tuesday in world geography they'd read about the smog in Los Angeles, where one of her uncles worked as an air force mechanic.

She tried to decide what the eye pin would be. Chrissy's drunk father. She held her wrist stiff and pointed straight for him. The ball hopped out of her hand and picked up speed. She could see where it had been at the same time that she could see where it was going. The ball blasted head on and pins popped up. The red neon sign above her lane flashed the word STRIKE. She pictured the sign flashing MARIE MARIE. The sign went blank.

Wiping her hands on the back of her jeans, she wagged her butt at Mr. Mustache, then turned and looked at Chrissy who was smiling straight ahead of her as if someone had wound a knob on the back of her head that pulled her skin back.

Marie stooped close to her ear. "Chrissy," she said. Now her voice was booming, really echoing. Her hands were sweating and her teeth tingled. "We gotta get out of here."

The sign flashed GAME OVER: Marie 165; Chrissy 97.

Outside, the snow floated down light and even. Chrissy stuck her hands in her coat pockets, smiled up at the sky, and opened her mouth.

"Let's hitch a ride to the ballroom," she said.

Marie watched the snow fall and collect on the concrete. It was dark except for the two lamps above the green metal door of the bowling alley. The junk lot in the field across the road was black, the wrecked cars denser clumps of black. Beyond that was Chrissy's house, and farther, the gray spire of the Saint Mary's church, then the water tower that said "Hello, You're in Church Grove," then Marie's house. Marie's hands had stopped sweating and now her head felt full of air, like one of the balloons that floated over her house after parades in Minneapolis or Chicago. Marie would stand on the back lawn waving, Hello Balloon!

A blue Nova pulled up in front of the bowling alley and Tommy and Matt Geiske stepped out. They were on leave from their army station in the Philippines. They hunched their shoulders and pulled their heads into the hoods of their parkas. They looked like two giant turtles pulling their heads into their shells.

"What's the matter?" Marie said. "They don't have snow in the Philippines?"

They hunched deeper into their shells. "It's an island," Matt said. "They have jungles."

One afternoon a few months earlier Marie had been fooling around with the radio in their living room and heard an interview with a man who had traveled all over Europe and Asia. He'd gotten malaria hiking around in a jungle in Burma near Mandalay. Now instead of feeling cold, Marie felt feverish and about to die, pictured herself and Chrissy weakly swinging machetes through thick green ropey brush.

Chrissy was catching snowflakes on her face. Tommy and Matt huddled close to the car looking at their boots, every once in a while checking out Chrissy's backside. Marie walked over and stood next to Tommy. He was about two heads taller than she was so she had to crane her neck just to see his chin sticking out of his parka.

"You wanna blah blah blah?" he asked.

Marie tugged at Chrissy's belt loop. "Chrissy, what did he say?"

"I don't know." She turned around and wiped the snow flakes out of her bangs.

"Well, look into his hood and tell him to repeat it."

Chrissy stepped up to him and squinted inside his hood. "Blood bath," she said.

Marie stood on tiptoe next to her. Tommy's head was deep inside his hood which was lined with yellowed fake fur. He had the thinnest lips she'd ever seen; under them a pointed chin stuck out like a ledge. Chrissy was right, his eyes were totally shot, his eyeballs getting a bloodbath.

"Gone to Guam," Marie said.

"Say it again, Tommy," Chrissy instructed. Then, " 'Car,' he said. 'Ride.' "

The back seat of Tommy and Matt's Nova smelled like pot and dirty laundry. The heater was blasting. Marie looked around the car for signs of the Philippines. In the middle of the seat, the stuffing bulged out of the vinyl; up front the radio and tape deck were broken. Chrissy pressed her open mouth against her window.

"What do you see?" Marie asked.

Chrissy shrugged. "Nothing. My mouth is hot."

Tommy drove down back roads, farm after farm swooping past the windows. The wheels hummed. Where the snow had been packed down on the road the sound was muffled, but when they hit a bare spot the gravel crunched and rocks spun up against the fender.

I can feel it, she thought. *I am moving.*

Matt lit up a joint in the front passenger seat. He held his breath and turned to them in the back seat, waving the glowing tip in front of them.

"Have you two beauties ever had Thai stick?" He smiled and looked at Chrissy, who was still looking out her window. His hood had fallen back from his square face. His buzzed-off hair was growing back in tight, bright curls that looked like meringue. His little-boy ears were pinned flat against his head. Chrissy toked slowly and handed the joint to Marie, who took a light hit and handed it back to Matt.

"Maybe you and me should switch seats," Matt said.

He stuck the joint into his mouth, reached back between the bucket seats and ran his hand up Chrissy's knee. She slid closer to her door and his hand fell onto the seat between them, as if his arm were dislocated from his shoulder. How long could he stay in that weird position? Marie had read about a Chinese acrobat who could twist her head behind her knees, lie on her neck and arch her back around like a table. She sighed, picturing herself and Chrissy curled around like that on tall red platforms, south Chinese tigers parading in circles around them, bleachers of Chinese clapping and roaring for them.

"I want to go to China," Marie whispered.

Chrissy pulled her mouth off the window. "Too far," she said.

How would the sky look from China? Marie thought about other galaxies full of spinning planets. She felt as if she could stick one arm out the window and poke a finger into Jupiter.

Matt was looking out the back window and sucking on the joint. Tommy stared at the road through the flecks of white, bobbing his head with the windshield wipers.

Marie put her hand inside her coat against her chest and felt her heart thumping under her fingers. Her life wasn't small, like the poem said, but dizzyingly huge. She picked up Chrissy's wrist and tried to find her pulse, but Chrissy pulled her arm away. Tommy and Matt's hearts must be beating rapidly, like drums, the hot island jungles flowing through their veins. She leaned forward so her face was directly in front of Matt's face. She could smell the stale pot on his breath.

"Tell me what it's like," she whispered. "Tell me about the Philippines."

Matt stared back at her with bloodshot eyes. "Lots of pot," he said.

"No. I mean, what does it look like? What does it feel like?"

He shrugged and took another hit off the joint. "I don't know," he said. "It's hot. We jog a lot."

Marie slumped back in her seat and shut her eyes. She kicked the back of Tommy's seat. She leaned forward and clapped her hand next to Matt's ear three times. The roach flew out of his mouth onto Tommy's lap. Tommy hit the brakes, and, as the rear end of the Nova swung across the road into the ditch, Marie grabbed the seat with both hands, sat bolt upright, and screamed. "Wheeeee!" Matt put his head in his hands, Chrissy's forehead hit the window with a thud.

While Tommy and Matt tried to push the Nova out of the ditch, Marie followed Chrissy down the gravel road, Chrissy walking as if she knew her exact destination. A car drove by and Marie turned and stopped to watch the shadows and fluorescence trail after it. Chrissy kept walking.

The snow was falling hard now, not in flakes but in small clumps pounding down on Marie's shoulders and head. The clumps filled the ditches and covered the road. The lowest branches of the trees were white and bent. Chrissy cut through the ditch into a field. Marie watched her feet imprint fresh snow. They could be hiking across northern China—"Tell us what is happening in the rest of the world," the villagers would say.

Marie stuck her hands in her pockets. Shutting her eyes, she held her face into the wind and took a deep breath—the Arctic breeze numbed her lungs. When she looked up, she saw miles of white powdery plains spread out before them.

Suddenly there was a sound like thousands of people mumbling. Marie stopped and tried to focus her eyes. About ten feet to her right Chrissy was walking slowly, her hands in her pockets and

Heavier Than Air

head hunched into her squirrel fur collar. Marie felt something on her foot. She looked down and saw a big, dingy gray turkey, and then two turkeys. She stopped and stared at them and they stared back.

"Chrissy, do you see turkeys?"

"Of course I see turkeys. We're walking through Kemper's turkey farm."

About forty feet ahead was a long white turkey barn, and they were surrounded by turkeys, thousands of shit-covered, gangly turkeys with red eyes. They walked forward, the turkeys walked forward. They stopped, the turkeys stopped. Marie broke into a run, the turkeys gobbled and trotted beside her as if they were escorting her, their rubbery necks stretched out, their wiry legs struggling to keep up, their dirty white tails dragging in the snow.

Marie ran over to a wheelbarrow that had been left in the field. She dumped the snow out, turned it upside down and stood on the top, balancing one leg on the handle and the other on the barrow's bottom. The turkeys swarmed around her.

"Life is big!" she yelled.

The turkeys broke out in a chorus of gobbling that rose to a clamor and then died down.

"No more school!" Chrissy yelled beside her.

"The world is ours!" Marie yelled, but this time she felt the fear in her voice. She scooped up snow and threw it at the turkeys, a field of blank red eyes watching her. Marie's heart beat hard. This is my life! she thought. A pain shot up her ribs and a gust of wind hit her face.

On the ground next to her, Chrissy slouched deep in her coat, her neck sunk into her shoulders, her long arms limp. Her face was the palest frozen blue. Who was she? Who would she be? Marie watched her cough and melt to her knees, then to her stomach. She stuffed a clump of snow into her mouth. Marie had a quick fear that Chrissy had gotten truly dumb like the turkeys. She slid off the barrow and lay on her stomach next to Chrissy, her neck weak as a turkey neck.

The wind was blowing snow into her face. Snow drifts puffed out of the ditches. The turkeys had stopped gobbling and were milling around them.

Chrissy's head popped up. Vomit booted out of her mouth onto the elbow of Marie's coat. She sat up and wiped the vomit from Chrissy's face with her fur collar. She touched her cheek. Even though her own cheek was numb, she expected Chrissy's skin to be warm, but it was cold. Chrissy's eyeliner had spread over her eyelids so she looked like one of those lost lonely girls on old movie posters who never go anywhere.

"Chrissy, remember that movie where Katherine Hepburn has a tiger?"

Chrissy folded her arms under her face, lay down in the snow, and went to sleep.

Marie pushed to her knees and shook Chrissy's shoulder. She stood and grabbed her under the arms and dragged her a few feet toward the road. But it was useless. She could never drag her all the way to the road, and even if she could, what then? She would have to drag her another mile or more to the highway. The road was empty as far as she could see. She pulled Chrissy's squirrel collar over her head. She lay down beside her and put her arm over her.

She wished she had the power to reverse the order of things. The turkeys would stumble backward into the barn. Chrissy would wake up, swagger to her feet, stick a cigarette in her mouth. Marie would follow her to the highway. They'd hitch a ride to Marie's house, lie on the braided living room rug, watch *Bonanza* reruns, eat saltines.

They'd go back to sixth grade, when Chrissy used to hang from the bus window as it rode up to school and shout, "My Marie! My Marie!"

During lunch hour they sat on the wide windowsill in the grade

Heavier Than Air

school bathroom, gossiping about the girls they hated and the international concert tours they would see when they were in tenth grade and hitchhiked around the world.

A loud high voice was screaming in Marie's ear.

"God, are you two drunk or what?"

She opened her eyes and saw a blue down coat open over a denim shirt embroidered with daisies and leaves. It was Sheila Kemper.

"What the hell have you two been doing?" Sheila yelled. "You must be freezing." She looked like she'd lost weight since the last time Marie had seen her, which was just this afternoon in the school cafeteria. Sheila's round apple face was hollowed out and her eyes were sunk in shadows. Even in her bony state her breasts bulged against the denim shirt and reminded Marie of a picture she'd seen of an Austrian milkmaid.

"La maison de Madame Durard," she said.

"What are you saying?" Sheila brushed the snow off Marie's back and then Chrissy's back. She held out her hands for each of them to grab. "God, we thought you were dead or something."

Mr. and Mrs. Kemper smiled at Marie. Marie smiled back. The car was hot, a steady stifling blow of overheated air. She and Chrissy huddled in the back seat with Sheila and her two brothers, who were holding their noses and staring at them.

"Where were you girls going?" Mr. Kemper asked.

"Dad, leave them alone," Sheila said. "Their ride got stuck over by the main road near the tracks, and they got lost walking across the fields."

Mr. and Mrs. Kemper looked at each other. He wore a red Russian felt hat that stood up square above his forehead. Mrs. Kemper wore a hand-knit scarf with bright teal blue figures woven into a yellow background. Mr. Kemper turned on the radio to country western and the car sped down the road.

La Maison de Madame Durard

"You guys are gonna have to wash your clothes, you know." Sheila spoke to them slowly and clearly, as if they were children. "I mean, they really stink, you know, like turkeys." She screwed up her nose. "I don't know how you could stand lying out there with all them. They poop in their own feed bins. When I'm filling their bins, they trample each other."

Marie felt the blood painfully returning to her fingers and toes. Her head ached. She was going to be sick as a dog tomorrow. She would wake up late and have to shovel the drive, then pull her brother in his sled to the neighbor's hill and push him down the hill and drag him back up. She looked over at Chrissy, who was leaning against the window with one hand over her face, crying. Marie had no idea what to say to her. She realized that this was only the beginning of not knowing what to say to her.

The two boys stared at them and made faces and pushed each other. The heat was crowding her; her skin felt pricked with thousands of pins. She sat back in her seat, folded her arms over her chest, and shut her eyes. Chrissy's elbow poked into her side and her raspy, broken breathing made Marie feel tired. She pulled Chrissy's arm closer.

Marie would have to go into the world all on her own—it was so unfair. She looked out the window at the lights of the town, the gray spire of the church, the water tower. She squinted and tried to see the hills behind her house, the hills of France. Then she tried to see the powdery plains of China. Chrissy was right; it was too far. She was only a Church Grove girl. Even as she thought this, her life felt small with loneliness and fear. But there was also a tinge of something else, anticipation, the miles of dark, dense space.

"So, where'll it be?" Mr. Kemper asked.

"Yeah," Sheila said, "where do you guys want to go?"

The Kempers looked at her, their faces round and inquisitive and smooth as hills. Marie and Chrissy looked at each other.

Mr. Hellerman's Vacation

MR. LAWRENCE Hellerman's brain is yawning against the slick coat of drugs the psych nurses give him to sleep. His mind moves like a glacier sliding south, leaving odd deposits on the landscape: a shoe burning in the fire, the eyes of deer like a trail of turds, work boots, hunting knives, bird feeders, the entrails of ducks and geese and quail. Squirrel bones. His father, Bernard, deaf, hairless, inebriated, slides out the side of the ice in a soft chunk; as soon as he's gone Mr. Hellerman can open his eyes. But Mrs. Hellerman and their six children are still trapped in there: the firstborn wearing a peach graduation dress, the three boys hunched over cigarettes behind the barn, the youngest girl, the baby boy. The unborn are there too, at the very bottom, scraping against his cranium.

Today is Mr. Hellerman's last day at Saint Mary's Hospital; Mrs. Hellerman and the boys have been milking without him for two weeks. Tomorrow morning at eight o'clock his daughter, a student at the city university, the first Hellerman ever to attend college, will pick him up and drive two hours south to deposit him in the living room of his father's father's farmhouse. Mr. Hellerman will nap before evening milking time. He will sterilize the milk machine, check the cows' udders for swells.

But today Mr. Hellerman is not a farmer, and all he has to do is pack.

The sun is a bright yellow winter sun. Lemons from Southern California, where he's never been.

He sits on his hospital bed, packing the objects he will take home with him. They are objects he did not take from home to the hospital: a stained-glass owl you hang from a string in the window (his father would have called it useless crap). A multicolored tea cozy he crocheted for Mrs. Hellerman, though they drink coffee, not tea. A birdhouse with "The Hellermans" engraved on the roof. A blue and white lap blanket he wove (the yarn soothed his fingers) the first week he was there. Mr. Hellerman wraps the owl in Kleenex from his bed stand; he wraps the other items in newspaper and tucks them inside the blanket at the top of his suitcase.

At lunch hour, his morning medication begins to wear off and he can feel his stomach lurch, what the doctors call his anxiety. Mr. Hellerman chooses not to eat; instead he pulls on a pair of loose-fitting gray slacks, a white T-shirt, black walking shoes. He walks down the hall to the stairwell. The stairwell is like a high-ceilinged cave. He feels larger in there, both large and small, the way he feels in the middle of Kemper's woods. And safe. He ascends in a quick jog to the fifth floor, turns, heads down the stairs toward the first floor. This descending holds its own momentum—his body pulls him down in a steady relief of falling. He counts his breath as it fills the stairwell, imagines it floats up to the roof of the hospital, where it rings like the bell in Saint Mary's church. Sweat drips off his forehead. His toes push up against the leather of his black shoes.

On his twentieth and final run to the fifth floor, Mr. Hellerman stops and looks out the frosted window. A gray path cuts through the truncated lawn, into a wooded gully. Today is the first time Mr. Hellerman has noticed the gully; before, he saw only the overgrown lawn that needed mowing. On the other side of the gully is a blurred space. A parking lot or an unclaimed plot of dirt? No, a freeway. He often has wondered why the homeless people in cities don't farm the unused land around parking lots and freeways. His daughter Julee has scolded him. —*To plant you have to own*, her strange round glasses sliding down her nose as she looked up over their rims. Before she went to college his daughter used to whistle show tunes while helping Mr. Hellerman hook up the milking machines and scrape the gutters. Now she says he just doesn't know things; he lacks any critical perspective, doesn't exist in sync with theories of material evolution and human society. He inherited the farm as did his father, but if his mind is chained to the barn and the fields, does he own the farm or does the farm own him?

The gully is dark, dense with growth. Oak trees? Birch? There must be a fence, keep patients out. Or in.

Mr. Hellerman wonders if he has outdoor roaming privileges at the hospital. No one has said; until today he has not really wanted to roam, content to sit in his room and listen to talk radio (never the weather reports) or walk the hallways and run the stairs. There was a thin man in brown slacks, always brown, who disappeared every afternoon for a few hours. His bed empty, the smell of cigarettes near the door of his room. In the evening this man sat in the lounge in a whirl of smoke, as if he were a magician, cigarettes overflowing two ashtrays, sometimes one-and-a-half cigarettes in his mouth at once. Mr. Hellerman pretended to do nothing across from the man, counting the number of cigarettes the man smoked down to the nub, cleaning under his fingernails with a flat wooden toothpick, waiting for the man, or maybe himself, to disappear in a smoke cloud.

That summer, the family had attended a performance at the high school auditorium: a man in a white shirt and pants put his hand to his forehead and saw the future. Does someone own a calf with three horns? Herman Voss stood up. Don't take the vacation, the man said. Herman nodded, as if he came to town every evening and sat in that collapsible auditorium chair waiting on advice. —*Where were you going on that vacation, Herman?* —*Nowheres.* —*Well don't go there.* Later the man hypnotized Mr. Schaefer, his daughter's math teacher, and got him to squat on stage and buck like a chicken to the roaring of his students and his students' parents. On the drive home Mr. Hellerman pondered an alternative future.

—*Wouldn't mind making my living like that guy,* and put a hand to his forehead, worrying did he turn the lights out in the chicken shed before he left and would Holstein 317 deliver her calf tonight?

—*You'd be good at magic, Dad.* The children agreed. They'd seen him make calves appear out of the loins of cows, make swollen teats deflate.

In the blur outside the window in the stairwell a shape appears. A deer, no, a fawn. Out of the ditch onto the strip of frozen lawn around the back of the hospital, stumbling like a drunkard on the ice, making Mr. Hellerman cringe. Crazy. What was a doe doing getting knocked up at the end of spring? Wouldn't be enough foliage, fawn would starve.

Mr. Hellerman presses his forehead against the glass and, shutting one eye, focuses the animal in his scope, tracks its movement along the ditch and then down to the wooded gully.

Bernard, his father, had tied the fawn to a bale of hay in the calf pen outside the barn. Lawrence stood in the shadow of the barn looking out at the fawn in the bright sunlight, its eyes like black marbles staring at him. It was the first time he'd seen a live deer up close. He was nine years old. When he was eight, his father had taken him hunting in the woods north of their farm; Lawrence carried a rifle and a knapsack of butter sandwiches and beef jerky his father had made. The rifle was heavy and sometimes he had to drag the butt in the snow and mud. His father shot a buck and Lawrence helped him lug it out of the woods to their truck; he clutched the hoof to his chest and heaved, but then his father told him to carry the head. Both hands under its chin and then just grasping at the rubbery jowls, blood trickling from the deer's nostrils onto his hands and jacket. The hide smelled like his grandfather's horsehair chair.

This small deer in the pen gave off a different smell, rank like spoiled cheese. Bernard spat in the hay and laughed. —*Pet him,* and pushed Lawrence forward with his boot. Lawrence stepped onto the hay and the fawn began backing into the fence, kicking out its front legs. Its teeth were white and tiny, like pieces of glass, and small clear bubbles clung to its black lips. Later they would guess the deer had rabies. —*Show him who's boss.* Lawrence frozen about a foot in front of the deer, his shoulders came up to its haunches. What was expected of him? Was he supposed to kill it? Suddenly, he lunged forward, threw himself at the deer, hugging its chest and wrestling it to the hay as the deer kicked and bucked. Lawrence wouldn't let go. Bernard banged a shovel on the deer's head at the same time that a hoof caught Lawrence in the groin and a terrible, black pain shot up through the middle of him; the pain was like a too-loud alarm ringing through his buttock, up into his abdomen, clanging in his skull. The pain did not surprise Lawrence at all; he recognized the sound as if the alarm had been there since he was born and even before that and the deer had just set it off.

Bernard smashed the deer's head until the fur and flesh scraped away from the skull and one eye popped out of its bloody cavity.

In the middle of the afternoon, while putting the final coat of paint on his second birdhouse, Mr. Hellerman has a vague thought, not fully formed, that he might like to sing. Singing would feel good, or, complete. —*When do you feel complete, Mr. Hellerman?* the group therapy lady's high voice. Odd, Mr. Hellerman never sings, not even at Sunday mass when his wife tilts her hymnal with the song in bold letters and notes in his direction, or when his youngest daughter, age six, smiles at him. —C'mon, Dad, in his ear. Mr. Hellerman likes to listen. But now, he doesn't know why, at the long empty table covered with last week's newspapers brought by Julee, the urge occurs to him. He opens his mouth and a note comes out, an ahhhhh, along with a gush of something he didn't know was inside him today. An avalanche of fatigue.

This this this, he thinks.

He picks up his paintbrush and dips it into the paint, the deep fluorescent green of the barley field at noon, between planting and harvest, nothing to be done but wait, a relentless gamble. What he hates about farming is what he loves about it. The roof of the birdhouse is a darker green, the front lawn in the evening as he looks out his living room window, rocking back and forth on the balls of his feet.

The lady who runs the occupational therapy unit, the unit that keeps him occupied he likes to say, is wiping off the tables around him with a diaper. She slaps the cloth against the blue enamel expertly; he admires her efficiency and the thickness of her forearms. What wrists! She is the wife of the fourth floor psych ward doctor, Dr. Horn, of all things. Dr. Horn's head seems to Mr. Hellerman to be abnormally thin at the bottom, making Mr. Hellerman wonder about the impossibility of Dr. Horn's chin. Mrs. Dr. Horn has a shapely head, and she pins back her long brown hair with a tortoiseshell barrette that catches the fluorescent light when she bends over. Most of the women in Church Grove, including Mrs. Hellerman, sport short, sensible perms that children can't tangle and equipment can't grasp. Mrs. Hellerman often clamps her bangs on her crown with a black plastic clip, an act that makes her forehead look white and blank and huge.

He doesn't believe Mrs. Horn has any children; yet she is not young. She got away with that. A light load.

—*Good afternoon, Mr. Hellerman,* when she gets to his table, her diaper waiting in the air.

Mr. Hellerman looks down at the letter P in the newspaper sticking out from the door of the birdhouse. Poultry $3.95/lb. Chickens to butcher at home.

—*I'd like to finish this,* nodding toward the birdhouse.

She stands there, thinking, and then she drops the diaper on the table and plops herself two chairs down. He realizes that he has been holding his paintbrush in the air over the paint can, as if from the time he looked up and saw her until just now he were frozen; as if, while the rest of him were moving forward, his arm stayed back in an earlier place. She must think him an odd duck. He feels his face go red.

It is snowing. Snow dribbling down since snack at two, peanut butter sandwiches and fruit cups, but now the snow makes a presence. Behind Mrs. Horn's head the curtains in the workroom are open and strings of snow—that's what it looks like—squiggle to the ground. Like someone is throwing streamers off the roof. The sky is having a party. *Goodbye Mr. Hellerman, so long nice to know you, hope you had a good vacation.*

Mr. Hellerman pictures his notoriously long driveway curving up their hill and pouring out into the barn (the wood will need a spring coat of paint). Tomorrow he will have to plow and shovel that, and the steps. Turn the heat on in the barn, if the boys haven't done that already. Close the loft off, drain the gutters, and check for ice blockages in the water pipes. He takes a heavy breath and sets the paintbrush down.

How does someone know to get a job like this? The first time he'd met Mrs. Horn.

—*I love the crafts and I love people. And you, Mr. Hellerman, what is it you love?*

And you? He kept hearing. And you?

Mrs. Horn closes her hand on the back of his hand, which has frozen in the air again.

—*You have a good return home Mr. Hellerman*, unembarrassed by the warmth of his hand.

Contrary to the heft of her arms, her skin is silky, reminding him of the down on baby chicks bought in cartons at Munson Feed. He had sneaked a few into his basement room where he slept as a boy. In the dark he lay under the sheet his mother had ironed and his wool blankets, the baby chicks hopping over his nude body. More like company.

Mr. Hellerman stares at Mrs. Horn's wrist and thinks of the word "stem."

The sky is white.

His shoe had sailed into the fire heel first, probably because of the angle of his kick when it left his foot. A work boot. A pair he especially liked. Brown leather with black shoestrings. This was three winters before the hospital, their last party: before the youngest boy was born, before milk prices dropped and his daughter's college bills began. Mrs. Hellerman was in the house, putting the kids to bed—before she went in he had kissed her on the lips and patted her behind under her parka in front of everyone: Leo and Janice, Arlene and Don, Dorothy and Alquin. The work boot smoldered, sending a column of brown smoke above their heads; the tongue of the boot caught flame. —*Say, Lawrence, you got one foot loose there.* —*He got more than that loose tonight.* Laughing.

Mr. Hellerman stepped away from the fire and cocked his head back and followed the smoke column up until it vanished suddenly. He stared at the sky, which he had taken for granted. It had been a long time, years maybe, since he'd looked up. He often looked out at the horizon to read the clouds for rain or strong winds, but not directly above him. He knew this because of the creak that stiffened his neck when he bent it that way, and the unfamiliar weight of his

Heavier Than Air

head. It felt unnatural, but of course it was the most natural thing in the world, to look up at the sky above your own backyard at night. Above the house and barn and sheds. Above the tractors and the combine and the huller. Above the wheelbarrows and hoes. He took another swig of whiskey from his glass. He'd heard that the sky looked different in the twin cities, you couldn't see many stars, a few, but not the Big Dipper or Little Dipper or the other thing he had looked at when he was a boy, the lion with a belt.

He looked up again and saw clouds of whiteness coming down; he could see the whiteness about fifty feet up, flakes descending en masse, their first snowstorm of the year. For a moment, in his drunkenness, he thought that the stars were falling, the heavens were falling down on him. Fear in his gut, he laughed at himself. But disasters do happen, crops wiped out, the farmer's dread. His grandfather had told stories of the locust plagues of 1879, sheets of grasshoppers dropped in a ten-mile radius and stripped the alfalfa and cornfields, the vegetable gardens, even the leaves off oak and maple trees. Lawrence's grandfather had opened the door the morning after the locusts arrived, the same door Lawrence opened every morning to put on his boots and go out to the barn. The grass around the barn was gone, bare dirt with only a twig or two of stubble sticking up. The fields for miles were bare, the most amazing nothingness he'd ever seen. Miles and miles of nothing so you could see the contours of the naked hills and meadows. The ground was a loamy black in some fields and had a reddish hue in others. He could see clear over to the Tool farm and beyond that even to Adley creek on the other side of the road.

—*Wiped out*, and a shot of plum brandy down his grandfather's throat.

In the backyard, Mr. Hellerman opened his mouth and snow wet the middle of his tongue. A few flakes melted on his forehead and on his closed eyelids.

Mrs. Hellerman pushed his side. —*Lawrence, what's gotten into you.* She handed him a shoe and squatted to rub his frozen foot.

When she stood, he looked down into her face, shrouded in the fur-lined hood of her parka, a woman with fifty-two quarts of tomatoes under her fingernails, not discontent, leaning on him the way she had leaned at the altar, toward him with her veil slung over her head and her lips, rouged red out of the ordinary, tipping until he was forced to catch them with his own.

—*I don't know what's gotten in me, Beverly. I don't feel so good.* He put his hand on her cheek and she turned away —*You'll have some hangover,* left him, not out of any particular meanness or pride, but in the practical politeness and confusion that had settled around the Hellermans, who knew when, like a small blizzard or winter fog. Mr. Hellerman sometimes thought they were born in the fog, there was something between him and the world, places beyond his farm were often shaded, as if he were trying to see forward from a gone time, or from a dark hole, the bottom of a well.

The curtains are closed and the hospital room is dark. He has returned from taking his four o'clock medication and is sitting in his underwear next to the radiator. The backs of his legs stick to the green plastic chair. He took off his pants because the room gets nice and hot when evening approaches. Artificial heat makes Mr. Hellerman feel taken care of, as if he just has to sit there and be warm, as if that is his sole responsibility. Two of the vents at the top of the radiator have cobwebs and Mr. Hellerman pokes a Q-tip through them.

At five o'clock he puts on his pants again and goes to group therapy, where he sits in a circle with three other people, an obese man and two thin women (he doesn't know where the others go), and wonders if he has any emotions today. The group therapy lady, Susan, wears a sweater with fringe on the sleeves, and she is telling them, again, about her psychological belief system and manage-

Heavier Than Air

ment procedures. Emotions are oceanic inside them, swelling into consciousness and then reshaping. They are to watch these emotions ebb and flow, they are not to cling, clinging distorts, and she looks directly at him.

—*Light and loose, Mr. Hellerman, light and loose,* her arms waving.

Mr. Hellerman pictures stray pieces of hay fluttering down from the barn loft, his youngest daughter tossing it out the door. —*You eat it,* at their dog.

Susan goes on talking; most of the time Mr. Hellerman isn't sure what the hell she is talking about, but he counts the number of times Susan has to adjust her sweater, the fringe of which, as she waves her long skinny arms in front of her, catches currents of air and sways.

I do not necessarily want to live, Mr. Hellerman thinks suddenly. A bargain: he does not want to live *with this.*

—This *being pain.* Susan leans forward, looking at him. Had he spoken out loud?

He knows what she says is true. Unavoidable. Not that he wants to die, but the weight of living seems unreasonable to him in this moment. The numbers: forty-two cows; three calves (one died he's been told); twenty-five chickens; four fields; six children; one wife. *And you? And you?* He counts the machinery, the two-acre vegetable garden, two sheds, barn full of swallows.

When it goes away he is hunting, standing back to sun scoping geese, a deer, pheasant, squirrel. The woods don't belong to him; he is weightless in his orange and green silence. And there and there and there. Silence.

His daughter, Julee, a junior at the university, wants to be a social engineer, or maybe she said socialist engineer; she wants to design alternative urban communities centered on trading and cooperative efforts. —*All for one and one for all,* and then she leaned forward on her dormitory bed and shaped these communities in the air as if

Mr. Hellerman had the power to see them, circles in the middle and circles around the circles. She had his wide hands, knuckles that sank in pink flesh. A long German nose set so startlingly low you almost gave up hope.

Later, while Mrs. Hellerman visited her uncle, Mr. Hellerman and his daughter played cribbage in the university cafeteria, Mr. Hellerman looking out the bank of windows onto a courtyard of concrete and benches. Not a tree or piece of green in sight. Depressing.

—*No, I love it here. I love the lines and the library and sitting on my bed reading books. It's what I always wanted, to be a real student, you know?*

Mr. Hellerman had always wanted a set of trained snow dogs and sled; instead he got a series of farm dogs, pleasant rangy mutts that followed him in and out of the barn and got run over in the driveway. The last book he'd read Julee had given him; a story about The Root Beer Lady who lived in a cabin alone in the north woods and sold root beer to hikers and canoers. —*Now that's a life.* —*Wouldn't you be lonely?* —*Only on Sundays.*

He moved four pegs into home stretch that gave him 21 points.

—*I'm out.*

The humanities building looked like a hospital, white walls, square rooms, speckled tile, long narrow windows. She introduced him to her anthropology professor, who was almost seven feet tall. In the middle of his forehead was a dent, as if his forehead were clay and someone had pressed too hard, or as if the two plates of his skull had been separated and then had grown back together. Mr. Hellerman wanted to touch it; it reminded him of the dent in cows' heads between their horns.

—*Your daughter is quite a thinker,* leaning toward him: is he bowing?

—*Yup.* And Mr. Hellerman found himself shrugging, collapsing under the words "p r o f e s s o r" and "a n t h r o p o l o g y."

Heavier Than Air

—She talks about you a lot.

—Oh?

The cows would be bellowing for him when he got home tonight.

—Yes, we're studying the history of agronomy-based workers, game hunters and tillers of the land soon to be extinct. His forehead flushes. *—I mean, in geological time.*

At first Mr. Hellerman heard the word "stink," but of course that couldn't be so—an educated man wouldn't say that would he? Extinct. And he smiled, for that's exactly how he felt, yes. Yes. A picture roared up in his mind of the saber-toothed tiger, the dinosaur, the Canadian grizzly. Yes. The Root Beer Lady had died and her cabin was now a tourist site. Let him pass, he thought; let the fields blow over, the machinery rust, the cows' bones sink into the loam; let the concrete roll and Julee's urban communities, with their gardens of neatly rowed beans and tomatoes and overpopulation of squirrels, spread across the earth.

Mr. Hellerman sucked in a breath, but instead of a laugh, his throat let loose a wad of phlegm and he choked. Julee pounding him in the center of his back and handing him a tissue, while Mr. Hellerman's eyes teared up—not from choking or in grief but in pride: his practical, hard-working, hard-thinking daughter. Yes, let her rule the earth.

At supper, Mr. Hellerman sits next to a woman who cannot eat without crying; every mouthful of mashed potatoes and creamed corn forces her to blot her eyes with her napkin. When Mr. Hellerman asks why she is crying she tells him a long story about her husband. She found him in their station wagon one morning a month ago, dead from carbon monoxide poisoning. Since then she cannot eat, or rather she cannot chew, something in her teeth prevents it, and she does in fact look thinner than most women he has ever seen, the kind of thinness that makes the muscles look ropey and the skin loose and tough at the same time, as if it didn't have much will to hang onto the bone.

—*He filled the tank and vacuumed the car the day before. His lips blue, like a blue lake. And his eyelids.*

And then she looks at Mr. Hellerman and draws her auburn eyebrows together. At first he thinks she is going to laugh, there is wonder on her face, the edges of her mouth turn up. But in a moment that changes and her face flattens and the tears stream out; he can see them exit the tear ducts inside the corners of her eyes. Mr. Hellerman is envious of this efficiency. He has spent many nights on his back in bed with a tear hovering on his eyeball, Susan's voice in his ear tying him to the ocean he has never seen. He puts his hand on the back of the woman's hand on the table. It's not enough. He imagines holding her to his chest, giving her the warmth of his flannel shirt and thermal underwear. He hands her his napkin.

After supper he returns to his room. The tiredness is gathering in his bones, the worry not far behind, a faint fluttering up his spine. He opens the curtains and presses his face into the windowpane; the cold seeps into his lips and the flesh around his mouth. The sun is fully set. The air is dark; he doesn't have much time. He puts on his trousers and shoes. He can't find his coat. Where is his coat? He takes the blanket from his suitcase instead. He thinks about asking the nurse about his coat, but the one on duty tonight has a nervous habit of talking if you ask her a question, her mind giving itself to you even when every expression on your face is resisting. Once he had made the mistake of asking her for a deck of cards and she had rambled on for twenty minutes about a trip she'd taken to Arizona last winter and how she could no longer tolerate the cold and how anyone who stayed up here was just crazy. The weather here is just crazy, she kept repeating, a bit insensitive, seeing as they were standing in a residential psych ward.

He takes the steps to the first floor. The stairwell feels different at night, going down, more civilized. More contained. Shadows and then more shadows. A strange severity. The lounge is empty. The big windows in front of the couches are black. The security guard keeping his back to him, keeping people out. He walks down a skinny hall away from the main windows and then down another hall and finds a beige door with an exit sign. He reaches for the handle, looks up—WARNING: FIRE ALARM. Down another skinny hall, stairs into the basement parking lot. Ahead about fifty feet, a green door, long rusted scratch across the middle. Garage entrance?

A woman is walking from her car toward him, head down, white shoes. An aide he recognizes as working in laundry; she'd dropped off his clothes one day. —*Door to door service, Mr. Hellerman. Don't get used to it.*

She is nodding into headphones, staring at her shoes. He grasps the green door handle. Cold.

There were seventy-five swallows in the barn that day. Winter descending. A long grayness, the longest he'd ever seen. And a constant clanging in his skull; he hadn't slept for two weeks. Milk prices down to eleven per hundred pound. He had counted every swallow that landed on the rafters and tracked their movements. Swallow flies to east rafter. East to west. North to south. He had an internal notebook.

From outside the barn. —*Lawrence, what are you about in there?*

—Counting, and a wave of his hand, a flip. Fall ending. Winter descending. Inside the house more numbers: six children and a wife.

—*Dad, it's supper time, come eat. The boys home from school.*

Forty-two cows bellowing. His questions circling the rafters: had he put the milk machine away, had he locked the gate, had he bought good enough feed for the chickens. His father would have turned his back on him. The fragility of the numbers he hadn't expected. Two cows looked like they had swelling, mastitis, the barn roof leaking, the pain clanging and banging. Where did it come from? It felt familiar, as if the pain were saying *Hello Lawrence Hellerman, you silly boy, did you think you'd never hear from me again? Did you think I'd leave you all alone?*

He began digging in his ear, his brain transformed into a thicket, crusty and sharp-edged.

—Dad! Dad!

Hitting his head against the barn wall, a thick oozing to release these thoughts and the fatigue, not enough room. If the skull opened he could free the swallows, skull pressing and a three-penny nail on the board by surprise.

—Dad *stop*, STOP!

And this this this. Blood was another surprise, the warmth of iron and salt on his cheek and in his eye, warm like deer's blood, his eyelid drooped with it. A cobweb stuck to his cheek and then a throbbing that was something new happening to him. He could understand this sensation, first sharp and solid and then transforming into a dense blast, and yet again into a numb weightlessness.

When he woke up in the hospital the next day the room was warm and empty and light and he was sliding through memories, but none he recognized, faces of people in magazines he didn't even know he'd seen, sounds of water and ringing. Julee was at his side, her strange round glasses catching the light so her eyes became stars. —*They did this to you.* Who was she talking about? She was quoting a book now, a book in front of her face. —*At the beginning is the scream, Dad. This is your scream.* What in thc hell was she talking about, he wondered, but he let it pass, she was young and full of ideas, he let the day pass into night, the windows black and without worry. Without.

Outside, the air was wet and cold. Or that when he breathed in, the cold filled his nasal cavity, and the small hairs in his nose turned icy.

He thought about the man breathing in carbon monoxide, his lips blue, like a blue lake. He crossed the service road to the lawn, his blanket on his shoulders. The grass was frozen and mostly buried under snow that did not look as white as when Lawrence was a boy. City snow.

He trudged across the lawn and stood at the edge of the gully. The fence was low, chainlink overgrown with snow-thick raspberry vines. Toehold in the thicket, he climbed over and slipped on his way down the other side, catching himself on a prickly vine.

Inside the woods it was darker, and quieter; twigs broke under his feet; he could hear the moss on the trees; he could hear the roots of the trees adjust to the evening as the earth shifts, closes in. He could stay here. Like a newcomer, he stumbled on a rock. The clanging bell underneath all that snow and sound and beauty.

A crunching sound about ten feet away. And this, not knowing he was looking for it.

—Hello little fella.

The fawn's mother nowhere. Mr. Hellerman stepped slowly toward it as it stared up at him. There was a cut down its forehead, a gash, like it had cut itself under a fence. Mr. Hellerman moved slowly forward, until he could hear the fawn's breath, and he reached out one hand and touched its fur. The blue and white blanket he'd knitted, his first blanket and the weave didn't turn out too bad, was tight enough to block the cold. He took it off his shoulders and set it on the ground. The fawn moved backward a step. Mr. Hellerman waited a few minutes, and then he stepped forward, delicately, kneeling on the blanket, and placed his hand in front of the fawn's snout. The fawn licked his fingers, tongue heat. It pushed its nose into Mr. Hellerman's palm, he stroked the back of its neck; he stroked and then he sat down on the blanket with the fawn standing over him, breathing just above his forehead.

The EE Cry

FRANK WASN'T sleeping at night. Instead, he sat on the living room couch and made lists of the new spring diets he and Barbara would start in the morning, like the six-day "Wild Rice Diet." You eat plain wild rice the first two days, the second two days you eat wild rice salad, and the last two you eat wild rice casserole. Every two months you repeat the diet until you've uncovered the real you.

"OK, this is it, you listening?" Barbara's voice was loud in the phone. It was the middle of the night.

"Uh huh."

"We fly to Hawaii, camouflage ourselves as tourists and fight the drug war."

"Colombia. I think that's Colombia."

Barbara sighed, "No no no, Colombia is for the lawyers. The new news is Hawaii. Boy, are you lagging. Now listen. We go to an isolated beach, we hang bags of ice—"

"Melt," Frank mumbled.

"Ding dong! Earth to Frank," Barbara sang. "Ice is the new drug, fourteen times better than crack. Anyway, when the dealers come we jump up, whip out our badges, and we become international heroes."

Frank pictured himself on the front page of the *Minneapolis Daily*, a white tailored suit and black tie making his torso look longer.

"There are no fat international heroes."

"We'll be the first. Besides, that's not the point."

"What is the point?"

"The point is there are plenty of things we could do with our lives besides eat."

"I'm hungry."

"So am I."

Frank had stopped sleeping at night back in November, when Jan, his wife, told him she was in love with Mrs. Herman, the woman whom for fifteen years Frank had thought of as "the neighbor lady." Apparently there was more to her hellos than being neighborly. On the morning Jan gave Frank the news the first light snow had begun to fall. That afternoon a long yellow truck arrived at Mrs. Herman's driveway and two long-muscled men tossed Mrs. Herman's dark wood table and stereo TV into the back. Jan and Mrs. Herman moved out of Golden Valley into a part of South Minneapolis Frank hadn't even known existed, where people rode bicycles year long and ate organic vegetables.

Jan and Frank's son, Dominic, had stayed with Frank. Dominic was sixteen, slim, and he slept just fine. An anesthetized bull swirling in hormones, Barbara called him. Frank heard Dominic brag to his friends on the phone about his mother and Mrs. Herman. "Yeah, the old lady's a dyke," he'd shrug. After Jan moved to the city, Dominic shaved off a half moon of his curly black Italian hair above each ear and started wearing T-shirts that said I COME FROM A BROKEN HOME. Apparently the girls at Golden Valley High School loved it. It gave Dominic the edge he'd never had before. It was Beth or Jean or Emily or Lucinda. Dominic would come home with a smile on his face, plop into bed, and wake up hours after Frank was gone.

What Frank lost in sleep he made up for in pasta. Fettuccini, linguine, pesto spaghetti, green pepper and onion lasagna with triple layers of ricotta and mozzarella cheese that salted his mouth and slid into the already large bowl of his stomach. There his enzymes churned the noodles into glue. The glue held Frank together, held his arms to his sockets, his head to his shoulders. Anchored him to his life throughout the minutes of his working day while he picked Da sounds from the Ba and Wa sounds of infants, trying to identify the nuances of primal language. This was Frank's lifelong search within the Child Development Department at the university. A purling cry with a single dominant vowel, he hypothesized, indicated need. He labeled it the "I need" cry on his charts. I need food, I need dry nappies, I need hugs . . . A roller coaster cry pitching up and down, aa-uu-aa, indicated general frustration. Then there was the harsh, full-lunged "EE cry," which indicated anger. Combinations of cries held their own, subtler meanings. It was these subtler meanings Frank spent his days deciphering.

He had met Barbara the day after Christmas—exactly one month after Jan moved out and began eating organic vegetables—at "Don't Worry—Eat Happy," a weight-loss clinic in Maplewood. Frank was the only man in the group; Barbara was the only Jew. They didn't last long in the program. The five-foot-eleven, 118-pound Fat Instructor insisted they count out 2,500 calories a day, dropping no more than two pounds a week: "You must learn to accept loss," she told them, and, "Shed gracefully and you will always fit your skin." She demonstrated by showing a bit of her own skin which fit her perfectly.

Barbara leaned over and whispered into Frank's ear, "Who's worried about skin, I want to fit into my underwear." He nodded, and they exchanged phone numbers and never came back. They started their own group of two and embarked upon a series of diets that were making the rounds that winter in the women's maga-zines. They began with "The Rotating Liquid Banana Diet"—three days of bananas, three days of apple cider, three days of bananas again—and ended with what they called "The Pancake Diet." You eat five pancakes with peanut butter for breakfast and five pancakes with peanut butter for supper. After a week you cut down to four pancakes, then three, then two, then one. For the final two weeks you eliminate the pancakes altogether and just eat the peanut but-ter. By mid-February Barbara had lost twenty-one pounds, Frank thirty-two and one-quarter. The day after the weigh-in celebration, Frank came home and found Jan's Toyota idling in the garage, and Jan and Dominic carting boxes of Jan's old psychology books up the basement stairs.

"Frank," Jan said. She reached the kitchen and set her box on the counter. Dominic rolled his eyes and carried his out to the car. Jan had a new haircut; her light blonde hair was feathered shorter on the sides than on the top. Her eyes looked amazingly blue. Around her neck she wore a raspberry colored scarf with blueberry swirls. She looked tight, healthy—edible, Frank thought.

"Frank," she repeated, and smiled not at him but around him. At his aura, at what she now called his "high density factor." "Oh Frank, you've lost weight again. Your skin is hanging."

Then she rolled up her sweater sleeves and with tight, tan arms, as if winter hadn't touched her, she picked up her box of books and walked out of the house. An icy breeze entered. Frank reached for a bag of stale potato chips Dominic had left open on the counter. As he shoved the first chip into his mouth he straightened his posture, smoothed the skin over his neck and, crunching, dialed the phone.

"I'm hungry," he said.

Barbara said, "So am I."

This time they went Greek. Salty spinach pie, chewy lamb, and baklava. Frank gnawed both his and Barbara's stalks of parsley. They drove through heavy snowfall to Café Latte for dessert. Frank ordered triple-layered chocolate turtle cake with sharp peaks of whipped cream. Barbara chose the steamed almond moo and blueberry tart. She dipped her crust into the creamy milk skin at the top of her glass. Frank watched the blueberries and thought of Jan. At the table next to them a couple in matching wool cardigans ate sesame noodle salad, whispering in discreet, well-formed vowels. Frank imagined Mrs. Herman kissing Jan at the bottom of her neck, tasting the pale mole on her clavicle until Jan lay happy and speechless in Mrs. Herman's arms.

"How's baby research going?" Barbara asked.

Frank licked the chocolate from his lips, but didn't answer. He was staring at the couple, who had slipped their hands under the table to form a bridge. Their fingers hooked together twisting over and under each other while their mouths formed a soft wet O. A purling cry with a single dominant vowel, he thought. I need . . . When the couple stood to leave, their plates were still half full of wild rice. Frank considered reaching over to take the abandoned food into his stomach, but the waiter arrived.

"Fat," he finally sighed. "I'm fat, that's why she left me."

Barbara dug for a blueberry at the bottom of her moo. "You asked her that?"

He nodded, though it wasn't really true. It was true that he'd asked Jan why she had to leave.

Barbara found the blueberry and dug it up with the tip of her fork then swallowed it. "Yeah, so what did she say?"

"She squinted at something above my head. Then she said: 'We're just not kindred anymore, can't you see that.' " Frank took another bite of cake. "I said: 'You're telling me we were kindred for fifteen years. Sixteen if you count making Dominic. And now we're strangers.' "

"And she said what?"

"Yes."

"Yes?"

"She said yes." He smiled and whipped cream dribbled down his chin before his tongue could catch it. Barbara handed him a napkin and finished her milk.

"What does Mrs. Herman look like?"

"Giraffe." Frank scooped another bite of chocolate turtle into his mouth. "With glasses." Barbara burst into a laugh, grabbing the napkin from her lap. Frank stretched his neck up and pretended to chew eucalyptus leaves.

The first meal Barbara and Frank had shared was Indian. She had pulled up his driveway in a lime green 1976 Volkswagen bug with the window rolled down shouting, "Dal for old souls." Frank stood outside his front door shivering in his size extra-large parka and stared.

"Didn't know VWs could run more than ten years."

"Hey, don't knock it," she said. "I bought the car the last year I was skinny and I'm not going to sell the damn thing until I fit into it again."

At the restaurant they sat near the heater on tapestry pillows and Barbara told Frank her philosophy on being fat. "When the scale hit two hundred I marked it on my calendar in lime green crayon and put my entire life on hold. The flowered midi-skirts I wore in my early twenties still hang at the front of my closet. Never mind that the fashions have changed, anything worth coming around once will return." Barbara thought in terms of when: when she was skinny again she would go back to school, buy a new car, fall in love. "Let someone else marry their fat," she had told a string of feminist therapists. "Mine is only visiting."

She had a Catholic friend who taught her about limbo, the between place where baby souls wait for judgment day. She knew this limbo to be her life. Not her real life, her floating life. In between being skinny and being skinny again.

Frank knew he fell into this space. Poor, nice Frank with his fields of flesh over his rib cage, his unkempt curly hair, his adolescent son, his gay wife. Frank with his sweet perpetual lack of enthusiasm, his kind monotone voice, his Da's and Ba's and coo-chi-coos. He had spent the last ten years bent over a tape recorder—rewinding, forwarding, plodding over the same sound day after day, all day long. His whole existence was a quest to hold on long enough to discover hidden meaning. Why did it happen? Because it happened, Barbara had told him. Shit happens. As the winter turned to spring, Barbara invented increasingly impossible schemes to fix their waistlines. Frank knew she was trying to divert his attention toward adventure. But adventure didn't happen in limbo, life didn't happen, love didn't happen. Limbo couldn't stop the shit, Frank thought, not entirely. It couldn't stop Mrs. Herman, it couldn't stop his hunger, any more than it could stop Barbara's clothes from shrinking or her job from being boring. That first night at the restaurant, as they had gulped down their mango lassis, she had told him she was a default adviser for an educational loan agency. Frank laughed. Barbara earned her living helping other people move beyond their mistakes.

In the last week of June, Frank and Barbara began their third round of The Wild Rice Diet, and Dominic began shooting a family photo essay for his summer art class. Frank and Jan were each supposed to choose three locations they'd like to be photographed in, and what they wanted to be photographed doing. Jan had made her choices and they'd done the shoot, but Frank was taking longer to make up his mind. The first was easy: he and Dominic sitting on the couch watching prime-time news. He decided the second photo should capture him doing his research. One afternoon he and Dominic hiked up the three floors in the science building to his office. Frank pushed the door open and switched on the light. Dominic stopped in the doorway.

"Wow, Dad, you're becoming an eccentric."

"Am I?" Frank looked around the room. Textbooks, loose notes, notebooks, audiotapes covered his desk and half the floor and couch. The only clear space was the window sill, where he kept a photograph of Dominic and Jan sitting on the couch eating sandwiches. Jan used to bicycle to the university to have lunch with him when Dominic was a baby and when the couch upholstery was still a royal blue, not faded gray.

Dominic was squinting into the lens of his camera, adjusting the shutter for the light. "Hey, I have an idea. You sit on the desk—like you're, you know, one of the things, part of the pile."

Frank trudged over to his desk, climbed on, and sat Indian style. His stomach bloated over his belt. He was sitting on years of observations that had led to very few discoveries.

Dominic stood on a chair in the corner of the room and aimed the camera down at him. The silver stud in Dominic's ear shimmered. "Look alive," he said.

As Frank was about to smile, a gas pain moved through his upper intestines, and his face contorted into a sickly grimace.

He remembered how, when they had begun sleeping together their freshman year of college, Jan had liked to tickle him in the small roll of flesh below his rib cage. She called it his roly-poly of love. She especially liked to tickle him when he was angry, which wasn't often. Once, Jan forgot to leave Frank's dorm key under the mat after leaving his room. He had to sleep in the hall because she'd gone to visit her parents in Church Grove for the weekend and the Resident Dorm Attendant was sleeping with some girl off campus. Campus Security could have let him in, but he hadn't thought of that. Monday, Jan came to his room to return his key. She didn't say I'm sorry. Frank thought she should. She told him he should have found some hot blond to sleep with. He yelled that she was trying to fob him off on some other WASP. That was when she started tickling. He fell to the floor and she straddled him, her hands digging screams of laughter from his stomach. She went too far. He warned

Heavier Than Air

her. Stop, he had choked out at least fifteen times, and then he started to cry. Jan jumped off and stood over him. "You are such a baby," she said. Shortly after, she left. Two days later Frank called her to apologize. She accepted graciously, inviting him to her room for strawberries and white chocolate fondue. She had seduced him with food from the start as though wanting him fuller, rounder. Once she'd cupped his nipple to her mouth forcing the fat and muscle to bulge into a chubby white breast. "You've got boobs," she told him happily.

"I'm feeling sick, Dom." Frank could feel the pile of papers slipping beneath him, and the room taking on a lopsided view.

"Just a few more shots, Dad."

The next flash hit Frank in the eyes and he went blind for a moment, the frame of the room flashing bright white. Then he was looking into a black hole.

"No. Really," he said. "I just can't go on."

Frank lay on the living room couch with the shades pulled down to block out the July heat. He was trying to decide what the third photo should be. Dominic needed the photo by next week. Outside, Frank's new newlywed neighbors were mowing their lawn and weed-whacking the overgrown path between their houses. As he listened, he pictured himself and Jan doing something together to represent the past, even make fun of it. A retro shot, Dominic would call it. Frank and Jan in their sixties wedding clothes signing the divorce papers. Frank and Jan in the orange coveralls they wore one summer to paint the house, only now they'd be stripping the paint off the house. Yes, he thought, they could laugh together, at themselves. Like buddies.

He got off the couch and found their wedding album on the bookshelf. He took one of the photos into the bathroom and stood in front of the mirror, holding the picture next to his face. If he lost another fifteen pounds he would be at his marriage weight.

As soon as he had this thought, his stomach felt unmanageably empty.

To Frank, marriage was the sound of lightly salted water on a low boil. Yet even in their early years together he had often had the feeling Jan was waiting for something better—someone with a lower density factor, lithe, yet big enough to understand her. He imagined it would be a tall blond man with no rolls to tickle or hold onto; a man she could slip off of easily. Frank waited with her. He waited for her to meet this man in her psychology classes, in her first job as a counselor, at the faculty parties they went to three times a year. He hadn't waited for Mrs. Herman.

"It's simple," Barbara told Frank on the phone. "We shave our heads and join an ashram. They teach us how to balance our chakras and block out all desire for physical gratification. We spend our days adrift in alpha waves, devoid of hunger, ambition, the lust for material possessions."

"Sex."

"What about it."

"I'd miss it."

Barbara sighed, "Frank, when was the last time you had it."

"October."

"October? You had sex in October, with who?"

"Jan."

Barbara was quiet. "She left in November and you had sex in October. But she was in love with Mrs. Herman!"

"Well, I didn't know that. Married to me. Sleeping in my bed. When was the last time you had it?"

"Nineteen seventy-six."

A long silence moved through the phone and then a slow hissing sound, almost like someone was wheezing . . . or laughing. Frank held his hand over the receiver while the tickle in his throat and belly worked itself out.

"You know, Frank," Barbara spoke slowly. "This is the first time I've heard you laugh in the six months that I've known you. And I really must say, it's one hell of an unpleasant experience."

The receiver clicked then, a tiny click that left Frank feeling hollow. "She hung up," he repeated to himself three times.

"Who? Mom?" As Dominic walked through the living room, he stopped to stare at his father, who stared at the phone. He was wearing some sort of musk oil that reminded Frank of deer meat. He looked up and saw the two moons above Dominic's pale ears. Here was his son, Jan's and his, healthy, handsome, getting laid.

"Feelin' OK, Dad?"

"Fine. Who are you going out with tonight?"

"Mary. You gonna see Barbara?"

"Barbara's just a friend, Dominic."

"Yeah, that's what I meant. Anyway, if you want me to stay home or somethin' . . . ," Dominic looked nervous. He tugged at his T-shirt.

"No, go. Go and have fun. I'm fine."

"Well, if you change your mind, we'll be at her house. Number's by the phone."

He watched Dominic go out the door with his ripped denim jacket over his shoulder. Frank's limbs felt loose. He headed for the kitchen. Pasta on the third shelf, boxes and boxes of pasta. He boiled the water with a teaspoon of olive oil, spread butter in a pan to saute garlic and onions. While he waited, he finished the bottom of a vanilla milk shake and a box of powdered sugar donuts. The pasta bobbed to the top. Frank scooped it onto a plate and added the onions, then more butter. He arranged the meal on the dining room table with a bottle of red wine. The doorbell rang. He thought it was Dominic, that he'd forgotten his key.

Jan stood with her hands folded over a package pressed to her chest as though she were meditating, or in a yoga position. She wore black cowboy boots, jeans, and a giraffe T-shirt. She stepped past Frank into the living room and glanced at the steaming plate of heaped pasta, and at the snowy powder glazing his chin and nose. She smiled. Then her eyes moved on over their oak shelves, the couch, the TV, the rose tapestry rug. The way her eyes touched the room—as if nothing in it held any meaning or said anything about their lives—made Frank feel lonely. His skin itched. He was tired.

Frank's voice came out gruffer than he'd planned. "What do you want, Jan?"

She looked surprised, her eyes widening. "I came to return Dominic's photos for his project. And I know it's not the weekend, but I thought he and I might— "

"He's not here."

Frank held on to the doorknob with a sweating palm. Jan stepped farther into the room and set the package in a patch of sunlight on the coffee table. "I'll pick up the last stray box, since I'm here."

Frank nodded and watched her head toward the basement stairs. He waited for the door to shut behind her and then he sat down on the couch and picked up the package. The three photos for Dominic's essay were on top. The first photo showed Jan and Dominic in soiled jeans with their bare feet propped on shovels—no doubt digging her and Mrs. Herman's garden. The second photo was of Jan in her new home, posing with a book in her lap on a new blue couch that matched her eyes. Frank leaned back on their old couch and took a deep breath. He turned to the final photo. There they were, Jan and tall Mrs. Herman with her long freckled neck. They were standing in a crowd of women next to a purple and gold banner that said Lesbian and Gay Pride. Jan's feathered hair was tousled by the wind. She was beaming and holding Mrs. Herman's hand, but something about the picture made Frank look closer. Mrs. Herman was looking lovingly at Jan, but Jan's eyes were focused oddly. She wasn't looking at Mrs. Herman, she was looking just over her shoulder at someone else. Frank followed her gaze into the crowd and saw a woman with long black hair holding the end of the banner and smiling back at Jan.

Jan's footsteps clipped on the stairway. He stuck the photos back into Dominic's folder and stood up.

"This is it," she said, and she sounded to Frank like she was singing. She carried the small box into the living room and studied the rug again. With the tip of her boot she ruffled the rose pile then smoothed it out.

"I wonder, Frank, if you really need this rug. I'll understand if you say no, but we . . . I need a rug and I'm short on money. I thought it can't hurt to ask."

"Does," he said.

She looked up, but not at him, over the top of his head, the way she had done with Mrs. Herman in the photo, the way she had looked past him or through him for fifteen years.

"Does hurt, Jan. Hurts all the damn time."

She studied the walls they had painted an eggshell white three summers ago. "That's not my problem," she said.

Frank's stomach ached up to his throat, where a cry burned. Not in front of her, he thought. Hold on baby, Frank, hold on.

"I know you're mad at me, but I am what I am, Frank. I can't change that for you."

Frank stared at Jan's serious, blank face. She really didn't know, he thought. And suddenly he started to laugh, he didn't hold back. He held his stomach and laughed his way across the room until he hiccupped and had to sit down on the couch. His body shivered from the raw inside to his tingling skin. When he caught his breath he looked up at the woman on his rug in his living room. Her mouth was half open and her eyes wide. She looked helpless. Frank stared at her, but he felt far away—from Jan, from himself—as if he were looking out from a half-sleep, from all his goddamn layers of fat.

He remembered a Saturday afternoon Jan had sat on the living room rug teaching Dominic to make owl sounds. "Who" she had said over and over. And Dominic had toddled through the house for a month afterward, imitating her: "Who who who."

"Take the rug," Frank said. "I'll get another one. I'll get two. In fact, take anything you want. Here, you want this pillow?"

As Jan left the house, the pillow hit the door behind her and Frank belted out a long EEE scream. Another pillow smashed into the window, another bombed a lamp which toppled onto the couch. The last pillow nipped the telephone off the receiver and it started to buzz. Frank slammed it down, then picked it up. He dialed the number that Dominic had left next to the phone. Then he called Barbara.

Frank met them in the driveway.

"Get your camera," he said to Dominic. Then to Barbara, "And you, you pose on the hood of that timeless car."

When Dominic came out with his camera Frank was sitting bare-chested next to Barbara, who was in her jeans and bra, on the hood of the lime green Volkswagen.

"So, Barbara," Frank said, eying her bra as Dominic got them into focus. "Do you want to go on a walk or something?"

"A walk."

"Mmm."

She looked over at him.

"Maybe," she said. "When?"

"Ready to shoot?" Dominic asked.

"Now," Frank said, and he picked up his roll of fat and looked directly into the camera.

Alfalfa

IT'S EIGHT-FORTY p.m. on a Saturday night and Ruthie Marie Hinnenkamp is not out driving around the countryside with her boyfriend John and her best friend Margaret in John's El Camino. She is not squeezed between John's hard hip bone and Margaret's fatted thighs; she is not lusting after either of them.

Ruthie is at home, on her belly in the middle of her bed staring at the mute TV. She couldn't tell you what she's watching; she is trying not to think. She is supposed to be reading her family's Bible and picking out the scripture to be read at her wedding. The Bible lies at her side. Her family waits downstairs. In one month, June first, before the Minnesota heat sets in full slaughter, Ruthie M. Hinnenkamp is going to marry John B. Koltser. The couple will move to the Koltsers' second farm about a mile down the road from their first. John and his dad bought it for them. John will leave his mother and father and cleave unto his spouse, and Ruthie will do the same. This is as her mother and father and sisters did when they were about Ruthie's age, which is eighteen.

"Don't be a baby, it's all worth it," Ruthie's sisters assured her after their special planning supper tonight when she excused herself with a headache. "You're gonna be a June bride."

John and Ruthie will be married in the Saint Mary's church by Father Leichen, a friend of Ruthie's parents and the parish priest who married both of Ruthie's sisters. He also performed Ruthie's, John's, and Margaret's first holy communions and, every winter since the third grade, blessed their throats against infection. The bridesmaids will appear in tiffany pink with big puffed sleeves and scooped necks, John will wear powder blue, and Ruthie will blind them all in high-waisted heritage white. Her mother and sisters picked out the patterns and the colors for all the dresses, except Margaret's. For Margaret's dress Ruthie picked a strapless curve-line, and a color the saleslady called crimson rose—Margaret is the maid of honor. Ruthie will walk in on her father's arm ten paces behind Margaret, who will lead the way for them down the middle of the aisle alone.

If Ruthie squints between the baby leaves on the elm outside her open window, she can spot Margaret's silo over to the left. From Ruthie's barn to Margaret's barn it's a fifteen-minute hike through the alfalfa field. Ruthie shuts her eyes and takes a deep breath, but she knows it's too early to smell any budding plants. After the long winter the ground will need more rain and softening for the crop to grow back as thick as earlier years. Twisting onto her side on the bed she switches channels on the TV, and her family's Bible slides to the floor.

Every once in a while Ruthie hears sounds from downstairs. She hears her mother's footsteps in the kitchen, opening the refrigerator, the gulp of suction before the door is yanked away from the frame. The family had already eaten supper by the time Father Leichen arrived to allot the details of the ceremony, but Ruthie hears the distinct sound of a waxy potato chip bag being ripped

Heavier Than Air

open. It startles her. She twitches on the bed because she thinks the sound is springing from inside her, from her stomach or her heart.

Ruthie imagines that her heart is a paper valentine with two identical halves—the kind she and Margaret used to cut out in school. They folded the paper in half and cut out one lobe, then unfolded it into a perfect crimson heart, like the one in the breast of Jesus. Ruthie remembers the time in grade school when Margaret was mad at her for something. While the teacher faced the blackboard Margaret dangled the valentine Ruthie had given her high up in the air, grasped the two top lobes, and then ripped it in half.

In her room, Ruthie digs her thumb into her breast until it hurts. She shuts her eyes again and imagines thick fields of alfalfa. She is ten years old and the plants stand almost as tall as her waist. She flops her small thongs across her yard and toward the path she has carved into the field since the beginning of summer. The corn and oats planted in early May have sprung up tall and healthy; the second-year alfalfa stems grow leafy and the tiny purple flowers on the ends have just begun to blossom. In the breeze, the purple tipped heads bend toward Margaret's house. Ruthie knows tomorrow her father will cut the field. She's been told that if the flowers bloom and go to seed the stems won't make good hay.

In his sermon that morning in church Father Leichen preached about insides and outsides. He told them that on God's scale, clothes count less than skin and skin less than what lurks under the skin.

Under her church dress Ruthie's freckled skin tingles over her bones and though she took a bath that morning and though the pure wafer-heart of Jesus rests whole in her stomach she feels grimy and excited. She's going to meet Margaret. In her plastic beach basket Ruthie has packed a cotton blanket, a can of Mountain Dew, a pair of scissors, two of her sisters' gold barrettes shaped like falling leaves, a pink comb, and her sisters' *Bride* magazines. The sun shines bright and Ruthie sets her basket down to pull on her plastic shades. It is part of the game she and Margaret play; they come in disguise. Behind the dark lenses Ruthie feels brave and the world becomes private and muted; she and Margaret are the only two in it.

The air in the field hangs damp and sweet with the smell of blossoming stems—but broken plants can be sharp, and Ruthie must be careful. She sees Margaret's taller, thicker body hiking across the field toward her and she waves. Margaret is wearing her floppy hat. When they reach their spot, far from the road and the barn, they kiss on the cheek and cling to each other's shoulders, pressing their flat chests together. Ruthie's chest grows huge and porous as a saint's—she feels as if she would suffer anything for Margaret. She unfolds the blanket and they settle cross-legged on it. Ruthie digs for her scissors and cuts out pictures of brides to tape to her bedroom wall; Margaret reads the articles out loud in her low, singsong voice. Later they comb their hair into the *Bride* fashions. Ruthie sits perfectly still as Margaret's square fingers part her waist-length sandy hair into three strands and tickle her scalp. The back of her neck tingles, her mouth falls open, and she shuts her eyes. She sees herself and Margaret walking through the purple field in white; the hems of their dresses are stained green and dirty.

Margaret teaches herself how to double braid, crown braid, and French braid on Ruthie's hair, and then she teaches Ruthie how to braid on hers. From the high heat of the Lord's day to the cool end when the sun turns white, Margaret and Ruthie flatten the alfalfa and braid.

Braiding is as old and clean as the Bible, Ruthie has heard her mother say, but when she returns home she takes another bath. In the hot soapy water she scrubs off her top layer of skin to see what lurks under it. She sticks her finger inside herself and pushes it as far as it will go.

After John gives her the engagement ring, Ruthie meets with Father Leichen. They sit in the small triangular room built in a corner at the back of the church. The walls are paneled and a fluorescent light buzzes over their heads. Father Leichen is a tall thin man with a sense of humor Ruthie doesn't understand, but she trusts him because he has a loud laugh that blocks out any doubt. His round gray eyes sit deep in his face as if protected by the folds of skin around them. Ruthie tries to look right at him, but instead she looks at her own sweaty palms in her lap, and then at Father Leichen's photographs of weddings and funerals taped on the wall.

Ruthie tells him she is confused about love. She tells him there are things inside her that no one ever mentions in the Bible. Her voice trembles when she speaks the words, and Ruthie can feel Father Leichen's round gray eyes stare at her small but growing abdomen and then at her throat which he'd blessed all those years. He thinks she is talking about the baby, but she hasn't even thought about that.

"There's nothing you can't tell to God," he assures her. "Nothing's too hard for Him to hear."

Ruthie wants to touch Father Leichen then because she knows he believes that; he can't imagine what she's talking about. She wants him to hold her. She reaches out and straightens the sleeve of her shirt. She wants to tell him that she would talk to God if she thought he was really listening. If she got any hint that he understood such things. There seems to be no way to get the words out of her mouth. Reaching over her to his desk Father Leichen picks up a half-empty bag of potato chips. Ruthie feels his teeth crunch, as if they are crunching her heart. He watches her and after a long while he sighs. Then, as if taking his turn in an old game Ruthie doesn't know they are playing, he reaches over her again and picks up the Bible. He reads to her Saint Paul's message to the Corinthians: "Better to marry than to burn," Father Leichen reads, and then he wipes a crumb off his vest, and laughs.

The summer when Ruthie and Margaret turn thirteen the sun rises high and hot. Margaret drives the tractor in her flowered halter top, tilling a fallow field for next year's oats. Ruthie perches on Margaret's barn fence and watches her. The steel blade of the tiller digs into black bottom soil and churns it to the top. Back and forth and up and down the field she drives. Ruthie swears she can see Margaret change color right in front of her eyes. The skin on her round arms burns from raw cream white to barn red and her long shaggy hair bleaches straw gold. Ruthie knows the feelings she has don't have anything to do with being fruitful; she knows she has to have her hands all over Margaret's burning skin.

One day they lie on their old red and white blanket in the middle of the alfalfa field. Ruthie combs Margaret's hair over to one side of her face. Strands fall into Margaret's mouth and she plucks them out and holds them up for Ruthie to grasp. Ruthie bends down to clip the hair at Margaret's ear and she dips her tongue inside it. Margaret giggles and bends her neck to Ruthie. Margaret sits still as the alfalfa while Ruthie giggles and licks her neck.

Ruthie thinks: chickens lay eggs, cows give milk, cats chase flies, and she loves Margaret Mueler from across the way.

When Ruthie's sisters turn sixteen they get boyfriends, and when they turn eighteen they marry. They set up their own houses close by, with their own family Bible and swing sets and vegetable gardens, and Ruthie convinces herself that she and Margaret will set up their own house: Margaret and Ruthie together forever, like Martha and her sister Mary in the Bible. Even when Ruthie's older sister has her first baby, and Ruthie starts seeing John, she somehow thinks she and Margaret will have it all, and things will stay the

Heavier Than Air

same. John will be her boyfriend, and Margaret will be her best friend. She never really imagines a life without Margaret.

It is Margaret who first points John out to Ruthie, the day after Father Leichen christens her sister's baby. John is in the eleventh grade and they are in the tenth. "John's growing up to be a real man," Margaret laughs when they are walking to town and he passes them on his tractor in his swim trunks and waves. Ruthie has seen him nearly every day of her life, but looking is a different story. The tips of John's dark hair brush against the top of his back which looks tan and flat as the road under her feet. That evening after supper Ruthie hikes across their empty cornfield to the edge of the Koltser barn. It is fall and the ground is just beginning to crackle. The lights are on. Ruthie hears top-forty music on the barn radio and she unlatches the wood door and steps inside. When the heat of the barn mixes with the outside air, the hallway fills with a warm mist like a layer of fog or breath. Through the dirty window of the milk tank room Ruthie sees John. Across the barn he kneels in the corner of the calf pen near the open pasture door, bottle-feeding a runty newborn. He sings "Stairway to Heaven" out loud with the radio. He sings off key and the notes float out with his breath.

John never pushes her in any way. They start going to the movies and sneaking into bars, and Ruthie is the one to get drunk and light her hand on his arm and on his knee. One night her hand drifts just close enough between his thighs.

Ruthie thinks sex with John will be hard but it isn't. It's as easy as stripping a field, she tells Margaret. When John is inside her Ruthie closes her eyes and pulls his hipbones close. She waits for the heat to reach her heart, the way it does when she's with Margaret, but John never goes that deep.

At school he is never one of the cool guys who brag and cruise around stoned in their cars. He is always shy and steady with big warm farming hands. Ruthie watches him set up the volleyball nets in the school gym. He plants one pole on the floor and then untangles the net bit by bit until he reaches the other side. In her room, at night, Ruthie thinks about the family Bible, and about Margaret's skin and John's goodness, and the tangled feeling in her stomach grows. Plenty of girls would like to date him, and after John graduates he asks Ruthie a few times to tell him if she isn't truly in love with him, to tell him right away and he won't be mad but just to tell him before it is too late.

"It's already too late," Ruthie replies.

The whole town says John and Ruthie are good for each other. He's patient, Ruthie's not. He plans, Ruthie doesn't.

John is always good to Margaret. The three of them hang out at the Greenwald bar or the sand pit or between the cornstalks when they grow tall. They drink Miller beer and talk. On the nights John picks up Ruthie and Margaret in his El Camino, they all drive around and around the countryside and they talk about the world until midnight. After Ruthie's third or fourth beer she lays one hand heavy as sin on John's kneecap and wraps the other around Margaret's waist. They take turns driving fast in a circle from Church Grove to Greenwald to New Munich and back as though someone were chasing them.

A week before the wedding John drives over to eat Sunday breakfast with Ruthie's family. After breakfast the couple takes a long walk down the pasture road. Not a drop of spring rain has fallen since the end of April so the soil lies choked and dusty and the oaks, elms and maples that line the road begin to look brittle. But the sky is one of those perfect skies, unyielding and blue, like Ruthie imagines heaven will be. She thinks how funny it would be if Jesus floated down over the pasture and scooped her up right then. Ruthie laughs out loud and John gazes shyly over at her bloodshot eyes and pale face. He takes her hand and says, "You want to marry me next Saturday, Ruthie?" Ruthie looks at the bulge of her stomach, at the ground, at the thirsty elms, at Margaret's silo and up at the sky. Her head hurts and she thinks about the passage Father Leichen read at Sunday mass, about the Garden of Eden. She says out loud, "The Bible says, Ye shall not eat of every tree lest ye die."

The Wednesday before the wedding Ruthie's father cuts the field. That evening Ruthie hikes through the broken stubble over to Margaret's house. The baby will keep her busy at first, Ruthie thinks, and Margaret loves babies, she loves anything that grows. Ruthie imagines herself and Margaret fashioning the baby's hair and dressing the baby in pink and yellow outfits on Sunday. Margaret has said she doesn't want to marry and Ruthie imagines she can come live with her and John on the Koltsers' second farm, and help them with the fields and the kids. At night, Ruthie dreams she and Margaret stand in a clean long pantry lined with empty jars, and they fill them with boiled corn, apples, and tomatoes. In back of the house they plant their flower garden with nothing practical the way they always talked about: just rows and rows of zinnia, snapdragon, Crimson Glory, and bloomed alfalfa.

Margaret is in her bedroom lying on her stomach on the floor. The bed lamp shines over her shoulder and her shaggy hair covers her face. A stack of papers sticks out from under her nose. "What are you looking at, Margaret?" Ruthie asks.

She hears Margaret inhale before she answers, quietly, "Applications for colleges."

Ruthie settles next to her on the floor and stares at her own sweaty palms and laughs. The room feels cold and she wants Margaret to put down the papers; she wants Margaret to hold her. "Margaret, who could teach you anything? You know everything."

Margaret doesn't say yes or no to that. She just wipes her eyes and sits up on the braided rug. "You don't have to do anything you don't want to do, Ruthie Marie. It's all your choice. Everyone here has a choice," Margaret says. "Everybody has to find their own way to grow. You and me, we both have to grow."

After her sisters finish reading from the Bible, they'll join her mom and dad in the first pew. When the ceremony ends John and Ruthie and their guests will walk from the church over to the VFW on Main Street and hang one on. Her sisters say it will be the biggest party this town has seen since their weddings. They invited all the aunts, uncles, and cousins from both sides plus neighbors plus school friends and John's baseball league. After the couple opens their presents, everyone will dance. Ruthie's dad hired a local pop band that plays the old stuff and the new. John doesn't like to dance, but Ruthie will stand on the VFW stage just like her sisters did, and every man will line up to pay a dollar and whirl her dizzy.

Margaret and Ruthie love to dance at weddings. When her oldest sister got married, Margaret and Ruthie danced the polka and waltzed until Ruthie's feet broke out in blisters. Margaret practically had to carry her home. When the other sister married it was the same story.

Margaret says it wasn't the blisters; she says Ruthie always drinks too much at weddings.

Ruthie's mother and sisters holler up the stairs and ask her if she is ever going to be ready. Ruthie turns her white veiled head away from the mirror and hugs against her chest the Bible she's to hold during the ceremony. She opens the book and stares at the black print. Before she leaves the room to join them she shuts the light off so she can't see the words but only the promising glint of gold on the edge of the pages. It's another beautiful day, and she glances out the closed window at the fields. June first and no rain means the crops will straggle up dazed and yellow. The first bales of alfalfa wait to be stacked in the barn. From where Ruthie stands, she imagines the smell of stunted, drying stems, and she hopes they'll make good hay.

Vegetative States

I STAND at my Auntie Jenny's hospital bed and watch her breathe. That's all she has to do—makes living look easy. Whenever Auntie Jenny forgets to breathe, a gray machine wheezes and feeds some mix of oxygen into her lungs. The air pushes her chest up and then her lungs slowly deflate. The machine breaths look the same to me as when Auntie Jenny breathes on her own. She looks like she's sleeping. According to my mother, sleep is something Jenny could never get enough of.

My mother and my Auntie Sal are sitting on green plastic chairs in the corner of the room playing five-card schmere. My mother has wound her rosary loosely around her wrist, so when she plays a card the black wooden beads tick against the table. Auntie Sal keeps her rosary wrapped in Kleenex in her coat pocket. Between the fifth and sixth games she wets a Kleenex and scrubs the corners of the windowsill and the crevices of the radiator. Though it's only October and the room is overheated, both women huddle in their coats as if they are freezing.

Five days ago, in the middle of the afternoon, while driving from New Munich to Freeport on County Road 52, Jenny lost control of the wheel and smashed her 1976 Chevy convertible into a utility pole. She flew twenty feet through the air and then her head hit a patch of concrete left over from when 52 was a highway. Since the accident, my mother and Sal, Jenny's older sisters by ten and twelve years respectively, have been staying with Jenny during the day and sleeping at the Holiday Inn a block from Abbott Northwestern Hospital. I told my mother they could stay in the apartment with me and Selsa, but they are afraid of driving back and forth through the city at night. Last year my mother decided to visit and drove up and down University Avenue for three hours looking for our street. Finally she stopped and called us from an Amoco station. Her voice on the phone sounded terrified.

Sometimes I picture her and Sal in their single economy room with royal blue carpet and matching drapes, huddled in front of the TV, sleeping in their coats, scrubbing sills and eating packets of beef jerky and Planters peanuts from the vending machines. They are country women—neither has slept in a motel before.

This morning, while Auntie Sal and I sorted through Jenny's mail, my mother bought two posters on sale at the gift center. She borrowed a roll of Scotch tape and a step ladder from the intake nurse and hung a dazzling poster of a burnt orange sunrise on the ceiling over Jenny's bed. She taped the other poster—a rainbow— on the side of the respirator facing Jenny's pillow. Under the rainbow, white calligraphic words read, *Lord, help me hang in there.*

I pick at the tape on the corners of the poster. I am thinking that the rainbow may annoy the nurses when they check Jenny's blood pressure gauge and oxygen levels, though they haven't complained. The bright colors and delusional cheeriness irritate me.

"Mom, are you sure the rainbow is necessary?" I ask. "We're not in Oz, you know."

Sal sets down a queen of spades. I notice how worn the card is, as if she'd been kneading the edges. "I told her it was a waste of money."

My mother picks up the queen. "Do you hear that, Jenny?" she says. "Our college girl says you're not in Oz." She sets down a run of three.

The next morning Selsa is banging around our bedroom. She opens and closes drawers. It's Monday and I should be studying anatomy, but I lie in bed, my face buried in the pillow. I hear Selsa say "Shit" under her breath. We've lived together seven years, since my first 4.0 semester as an undergrad, and this banging and cursing are new for her, like this lying in bed is new for me. She sits on the side of the bed and rests her hand on the back of my neck. "You are the slug of my heart," she says. "But have you been wearing my underwear?"

I don't answer. She sighs and gets up.

The clothes on the floor of our room are piling up, weeks of Haines underwear, cotton socks, slacks, button-down shirts. All mine. Along the wall near the bed and in the corners, piles of books gather dust: *Physical Chemistry, Gray's Anatomy, The Physiology of Ten Major Diseases, Your Skeletal System.*

On August first I started my second year of medical school at the University of Minnesota. Last year I recorded all the lectures and listened to them twice. I spent weekends in the library, ran five miles every morning, cooked supper three times a week, slept four hours a night. During winter holiday and summer, I slogged baskets of French fries to high school students every day from noon to two a.m. at Embers on Hennepin Avenue. When school started six weeks ago, I took out a bread-and-butter loan and quit my job. I quit running, cooking, picking up clothes.

Through the pillow I hear Selsa's silk skirt swish down the hall. The front door opens. "Deborah, you've got twenty minutes to get ready for classes." She pauses. I hear the door close.

I am thinking about my death; I am wondering if death hurts, what it feels like. I imagine the moment of death itself, and then, of course, after. I know this is pointless, unreasonable. I roll over in the sunlight, put the pillow over my face and hold my breath. My heart thumps dimly against my upper ribs. The carbon dioxide waiting for exhale presses against my cranium, my diaphragm, the roof of my mouth. My hands tingle. My ears buzz. But I hear no loud protests, no wild clamoring from my inner soul. It's all very quiet.

Death feels familiar somehow. As though I've already been there. Death is a mindless, reassuring drone. A dark luminous hum. A buzz.

I have seen dead bodies. I have sliced open abdomens, identified the bluish crest of the ilium, dissected the rectum. I have divided the reptilian R-complex of the brain from the mammalian limbic system from the primatial neocortex. The day before my mother called from the hospital to tell me Jenny had crashed, I stood in my blue gown in the dissection room and held lungs in my hands.

In my top dresser drawer next to our bed there is a bottle of sleeping pills I got last year when I had insomnia. Now I sit up in the sunlight, take out the bottle and read the label. I drag the phone from the hallway to the bed and call the medical library. The librarian is very sweet; she is sipping coffee and chewing on something. I ask her about the physiology of barbiturate intake and tell her I am studying to be a doctor. She tells me good luck. She finds a book on pharmacodynamics and explains in a factual voice that barbiturates selectively depress an area in the medulla oblongata which regulates respiration and heart rate. The excitable cells in your brain relax.

"The body falls into a sleeping state," she says. "Not a normal sleep, but a sleep uninterrupted by dreams."

"What happens with overdose?" I ask.

She hesitates. "The lungs give out; the esophagus closes in."

I close my eyes and imagine the afterlife as a clean room—my eyelids are a white wall. I imagine walking across this room and crawling into a wide bed between freshly washed sheets. I pull the top sheet up to my chin, lay my head back on the white pillow. I rest my hands at my sides. The shades in the room are drawn but the windows are open. A slight breeze touches my shoulders and face. I close my eyes and think of nothing. I breathe in and out.

That afternoon at the hospital my mother is hovering over Jenny's bed. Jenny opens her eyes and stares at the ceiling where my mother hung the sunrise. She closes them. She has been doing this for two days. Sal looks out the window at the gray paved top of the Sears building. Just before I arrived she had hand-washed Jenny's underwear and nightgowns in the sink because she doesn't trust the laundry to return them. The items now hang over the radiator.

"Jenny, who am I?" my mother asks. She waves her hand and the rosary back and forth in front of Jenny's face.

I sit on the end of the bed. "Amazing what we expect from the comatose," I say.

"The doctor says she's not in a coma anymore," my mother says. "She's in a vegetative state." She pronounces the words clearly.

"What's the difference?"

She raises her eyebrows at me as if to say, You're the medical student. "Coma is like sleeping," she says. "Now she's not sleeping, but she's not awake. Don't you have classes today?"

I shrug.

My mother explains that, according to the doctor, the swelling in Jenny's brain has gone down enough for her to resume consciousness. The fact that she hasn't may imply that her brain has gotten used to the nonactive state; the normal chemical reactions aren't kicking in. But the doctor says it's more likely she's vegetative. Her reptilian trunk and mammalian midbrain coordinate enough to tell her heart to beat and her lungs to respire. But the frontal and

Vegetative States   111 parietal lobes—her memory, thinking, and knowing parts—are permanently damaged.

"We can't know how the brain will grow," my mother says. "It's possible that with prayer and time the damaged parts will repair themselves and branches of her brain will bloom back to life."

"I'm not sure you can talk about Jenny's brain as if it were a bush tomato plant," I say.

In the visitors' lounge my mother puts two quarters in the vending machine. A young man in a hospital gown sits on the only couch, drooling and staring at a TV commercial. Once when I was in the sixth grade, I woke in the night and walked into the kitchen for a glass of milk. My aunts and uncles were sitting around our kitchen table eating nuts and playing schmere. Jenny stood next to the refrigerator talking to my mother while she fixed butter sandwiches. I yanked on the end of the red belt Jenny had tied too tightly around her waist. "Who was the second president of the United States?" I quizzed. Jenny's face got red. She looked from me to my mother to the table and back. "I don't know," she said. "Herbert Hoover?" She threw her head back and laughed at herself; then we all laughed.

"Do you think Jenny would want to wake up without her thinking intact?" I ask. "I mean, her brain was never exactly blooming."

My mother glances at me. She smacks the vending machine and the bag of peanuts falls loose. "No, she was never smart, that wasn't her gift," she says. "But who's to say God values smart more than anything else?"

I put my quarters in the slot and a Hershey bar slides out. "Well, maybe she just wants to get the whole damn thing over."

My mother opens her bag of peanuts. She spills a few into her palm. She stares at them. "I have more faith in Jenny than that," she says.

That evening, other relatives arrive. They step shyly into Jenny's room, hang back in the doorway: two towheaded teenage second cousins and an older man my mother reminds me is my great-uncle. They stand in the middle of the room with their arms at their sides and look at the floor. My mother and Sal give them a tour of the respirator, the glucose IV, the I&O chart.

We sit around Jenny's bed on the green plastic chairs. The two boys are sipping Cokes. The television is blasting.

"She was not wearing her seat belt," Sal leans forward and whispers. The visitors shake their heads.

"A man from Greyeagle once was pinned inside the car by the seat belt and became paralyzed from the neck down," my great uncle says. "It happens. You can't always tell."

My mother and Sal look at each other. "I suppose so," they say.

After the relatives leave, Sal tells me this man's oldest son, a brother of the towheads, once had shut himself in the garage with the car running.

"Did he die?"

"Oh no. Alquin found him and the next afternoon the boy was back on the tractor." She plucks Jenny's undergarments from the radiator and gives them a shake.

My mother and Sal believe that if Jenny had been wearing her seat belt she would not have flown and hit concrete but would have stopped with the passenger side of the Chevy hugging the pole in the ditch. Now as they sit in their chairs and deal out cards, they tally up the potential damage—broken ribs, legs, even a snapped vertebra—and weigh all this against the vegetative state. They pull their coats closer, pray, shake their heads and click their tongues. They are women who gutted chickens and pigs before they learned to read; who at eleven and thirteen picked two acres of beans, put up fifty-six quarts of cabbage and tomatoes, baked eleven loaves of bread in a day. They raised Jenny. For them life is a series of small responsibilities dealt out by and owed to God. Shirking their duties, even through death, would never seriously occur to them.

On the way home I run a red light and a Jeep almost hits me. I pull onto the shoulder and lay my head on the steering wheel. I listen to the sighs of the radiator. I think about my skeletal system and the tired gray matter inside my skull. I think about how fragile a brain is.

Selsa is cooking biryani and spicy sweet potato pie. She is trying to draw me back into my life. Last week she brought home a bottle of fresh-squeezed orange juice and a piece of almond cheesecake every night. The five boxes of cake are stacked in the fridge; half of the juice has turned acidic. She asks me if I'm hungry and I shake my head.

"Excuse me, doctor, I can't hear you," she says. "Could you try using language."

I ignore her and open the vegetable bin. I take out a head of broccoli and go into the bedroom.

Selsa has made the bed. She has also folded some of my shirts and pants and set them on the edge of the bed for me to put away. I set the broccoli on my pillow. I pull the covers up over the stalk so the green head sticks out. I feel Selsa's hand on my shoulder.

"This is what our children will look like," Selsa says.

In the kitchen, I hold a wooden spatula in my mouth to keep from crying, I cut up eggplant and red onions. Selsa fries the vegetables in olive oil. We eat at the kitchen table and I stare out the window. The sky is gray. When I was little my mother told me God's kingdom was behind the sky. I imagined the back of our sky was heaven's floor. Jesus walked in a white robe with his disciples. Moses and Joseph of the coat of many colors hung out at wells and rode camels. I never doubted that they were there, and that it was enough that I would someday join them. Then I learned that the sky is composed of gases, the clouds are nothing but water vapor, and the blue is only a refraction of sunlight.

Perhaps our energy seeps out of us when we die. Perhaps the protons and neutrons from our cells leak back into the atmosphere and feed something.

But I am not thinking about the afterlife or Jenny when I look at the sky from the kitchen table tonight. I am thinking about the body itself. I know what it contains, but what makes us alive? This is what I want to ask someone. But I wouldn't trust anyone's answer.

After dinner, Selsa watches TV and I lie in bed next to the broccoli. I picture my second cousin crouched in the back seat of my great-uncle's Pontiac. Wisps of his white blond hair stick to the plastic seats, the exhaust drifts in the dusty back window, and his tissues and organs turn a deep, restful blue.

The next afternoon I pack one of the blankets from my bed into the Toyota. I think of Selsa and throw in one of the bottles of orange juice that's still good.

At first I don't know where I'm going, but then Interstate 94 turns into suburbs, then into familiar yellow ditches, low hills, Holsteins, fallow cornfields. The New Munich exit ramp has been repaved.

I park the car across from the utility pole on the shoulder of County Road 52. I spread the blanket on the side of the ditch. I drink my orange juice and stare at the few cars that pass. The air is still and cool.

I lie on my back. I am wearing a short-sleeved shirt and the little hairs on my arms tingle. Ants crawl up my neck. Horseflies and mosquitoes that have somehow lived through the cool beginning of fall buzz.

I grew up on this land. It's flat and brown now that the leaves have lost their chlorophyll. But in the spring the green is brilliant. And even now I imagine the birch and maple forests behind the fields show hints of bursting into red.

The short yellow grasses around the utility pole are flecked with the blue paint and rust from Jenny's Chevy. I stand with my back to the pole, facing Freeport. I count twenty paces.

There is a brown stain the size of a grapefruit on the old concrete. Squatting next to the stain, I trace the blurred outline. A strand of short dark hair sticks up from a crack in the concrete. I put the hair in my pocket.

Selsa's voice booms on the answering machine. She's at work. "Deborah, where are you? I called your mother at the hospital and she says you haven't been there, and your professors from school called this afternoon and said you better get your butt to some classes next week. If you're home, I want you to pick up the phone." I hear not only the anger in her voice, the frustration, but also the fatigue. "I'm sick of this, you asshole." She slams down the phone.

From the floor I pick up the rest of the shirts and pants and underwear, fold the clean ones and put them in drawers. I put my school books in a paper bag. I set the bag behind the shoes in the hall closet and take out the duster. I wipe off all the surfaces in the room. I sweep the floor.

The sheets feel cool under my chin. The ceiling is bare. I open the bottle of pills and pour them onto my chest. I count fifteen. I swallow one and then two. I picture my medulla oblongata and all the cells in my brain kicking back and relaxing. I think about swallowing more pills, the esophagus closing in. Then I see my mother at the hospital. She is climbing the ladder she'd borrowed from housekeeping. She's wrestling with an armful of posters, tape tangled in her hair, the roll of tape between her teeth. Despite myself I laugh.

The doctor lifts Jenny's hand high into the air and lets go, and the arm falls heavily to her chest. He asks her to blink; she stares straight up at the ceiling. He sticks a long pin into her toe, and her foot twitches. Only a reflex, the doctor tells us.

Tomorrow the doctor, my mother, and some of the other relatives are going to have a big powwow in the third-floor conference room of the hospital. I am not immediate family—husband, daughter, sister—so I am not invited or expected to participate, which is a relief. They must decide how long to keep Jenny on the respirator. The doctor sees no sense in pretending that science, in this case, can do more than maintain a body in a hospital bed. Auntie Sal, always mindful of waste, has already given her opinion: the body is made for work; shut the thing off. If they turn the respirator off, chances are slim that Jenny's brain will kick in and she'll breathe on her own. But it is possible.

There are rings around my mother's eyes, deep gray rings. She looks tired. Sal drove home two days ago to her farm and her chickens and my Uncle Ralph. My mother wants to leave too—she has spent more money than she had all year, she misses my father, she is in the middle of a quilt. This waiting has become tedious. She sighs and picks at a fruit cocktail on the tray the nurse mistakenly dropped off for Jenny.

"Where were you yesterday?" she asks. "Selsa says you haven't been going to your classes. She says you're sleeping all the time."

"I went to the crash site."

My mother squints and looks at me, baffled. She shakes her head as if I told her I'd painted myself green and run naked down University Avenue.

She wipes her mouth on her napkin and stuffs it inside the plastic cup. She holds up a Styrofoam bowl. "Soup?"

"Nobody likes hospital food, Mom."

"You did. At the end of seventh grade when you were in the hospital you told me that you loved the soup and the desserts."

I don't remember much about being in the seventh grade or being in the hospital. I remember stomach aches, and just before finals staying home from school for a month. I lay in my bed reading one book over and over. This woman travels from her childhood home in Michigan to the Himalayas and single-handedly nurses a village of poor people who are dying of typhoid. I would read to the end of the book and feel this horrible pressure in my stomach. I felt terrified of having to get up and dressed and start the day. I would turn back to page one and start the book again.

"What was wrong with me?" I ask.

My mother looks down and sips more of the soup. "The doctors said they didn't know."

"Are you sure it was me? Maybe it was Kay or Susan."

"No, it was you," she says quietly. "Looking back, I think you may have been depressed."

I expect my mother to look away when she says this—or rather, I don't expect her to say this at all—but she has and she doesn't. She looks right at me and doesn't blink. In fact she looks a little relieved.

"Deborah, do you think you're the only one in the world who's ever felt sick and tired of things?"

"Why didn't you do something?" I ask.

"I did. I brought you to the hospital."

"You should have taken me to a counselor."

"I know that now," she says. "Everyone knows about depression now. You think I'm a dummy?"

She opens her purse and starts to rummage. "Here. Have a piece of gum."

The cinnamon flavor of Big Red shoots through my mouth.

"I just wish she'd do something," she says, and I know she's referring to Jenny. "It's just so sickening to see her lie there like that. Yesterday I was sitting next to her bed and I just threw up my arms." My mother throws up her arms and lets them drop to her sides. "Goddammit, Jenny," she yells. "Stop being so damned self-centered. Shit or get off the pot." She looks toward the door to see if someone is listening.

My mother sighs and leans over the hospital bed until her face hovers above Jenny's face. She takes her hand. "Jenny," she says. "You've got to make up your mind. The living or the dead."

My mother and the relatives are in the conference room deciding. Her rainbow hangs on the respirator, her sunrise on the ceiling.

The muscles in Jenny's face are going slack, as if her face is slowly spreading across the pillow. She looks rubbery and pale compared to when she first came in. Her eyes are wide open now, even at night. But they are glazed, unfocused, like fish eyes. For every five breaths the machine puts in her she takes one or two.

Everyone has brought fall flowers from their yards and gardens. Mums, purple sedums, zinnias. There are also the orange and yellow marigolds Selsa and I brought yesterday, the strawflowers from Sal's front yard which she sent with one of the brothers, the bloomed petunia plant my mother bought at the gift center. The room smells like plants and earth and cooked air.

I imagine a miracle. Even knowing that her brain is squeezed and bruised, I picture Auntie Jenny sitting bolt upright and speaking. Not the laughing self-deprecating speech of the real Jenny but long elegant sentences. I imagine her as an oracle, someone straddling life and death, possessing the knowledge that would end all the mystique and uncertainty and delusions about the meaning of our lives and why we go on living them. The bruises on her temples have faded, but a luminous gray color deepens around her eyes.

I have so many questions. What is it like not having to think about anything, living in a half-state? What does it feel like when you know you are going to crash, to see that pole in front of you and feel your head finally hitting the concrete? What in the world will I do with my life if I can't make it through medical school?

I kneel down at the side of Jenny's bed and rest my arms on the mattress. My breath tastes stale and metallic. I hear a noise and look up. It's only air moving through her upper intestines.

I envy her, not because she will die, necessarily, but because she doesn't have any more questions. She is removed from all this bright, insistent, blooming survival.

I can feel myself careering through the air.

"Jenny," I whisper. Her eyelids flutter, or it could be only my breath against them.

Mother

FROM WHERE she sits at the desk in her bedroom, Deborah can hear her mother, who has been camped on the living room couch for three days, nibbling saltines. The low hum of the soap operas, even though Deborah has insisted she wear headphones, penetrates the walls and Deborah's skin. None of it is fair. She picks up her pen and writes on yet another blank page of her dissertation the words *ego regression*. Then she writes *Selsa Basu doesn't love me anymore.*

No, it isn't fair, she thinks: her girlfriend's sudden departure with the birdlike English professor after ten years of Deborah's devotion (or was it Selsa's devotion?); Deborah's mother flying in from Minnesota for her only visit to San Francisco in six years (after Deborah's middle-of-the-night plea for who-knows-what-kind of mothering) only to be greeted by a daughter who hadn't changed out of her pajamas for three days and who now wishes more than anything that her mother would go home.

Later in the afternoon her mother puts on her pink plastic

visor—the same one she's been wearing since Deborah's childhood—and stands at the door to the bedroom. "Deborah, isn't it time to go?" she asks.

On the 21 Hayes bus her mother holds on to the metal rail on the seat in front of her and says the street names out loud: Cole, Steiner, Masonic, Divisidero. Deborah can tell she is quite proud of herself. Until three days ago her mother had never been on a city bus, or even in the streets of a city bigger than Saint Cloud, which is an hour from the small town where Deborah grew up and where her mother still lives with her father in a house surrounded by barley fields. Now, not a minute goes by without some question about San Francisco that Deborah, who made the city her own with Selsa six years ago, must answer.

"Where is Golden Gate Bridge from here?" her mother asks, craning her neck to look out the back window.

Deborah shrugs. As a teenager she despised her mother's obstinate denial of anything difficult or dark. Now, as her mother smiles at all the passengers, she envies her perpetual good nature and childlike curiosity. Yesterday on the bus, Deborah leaned her head against her mother's shoulder—not the full weight, but tentatively resting there. Her mother let out a nervous little laugh, patted Deborah's arm, and then asked her to identify all the funny-looking puffball trees in the Panhandle.

"The bridge must be that way," she says now. "Are we going east?"

"I think so, Mom. I don't know."

Her mother digs in her pocket and hands Deborah a tissue that looks like it has been living in her jacket for a long time. Her other hand grips the rail, her mouth forming yet another question. She came to help, but Deborah suspects she also just wants to be a tourist and see the city. Every morning, before Deborah awakens, her mother quietly dresses in her flowered skirt and a pastel shirt and walks up the hill to the famous Saint Ignatius Church at the

Heavier Than Air

Jesuit university. In the afternoons the two of them go apartment hunting; without Selsa's professorial salary, Deborah can't afford the one bedroom with a windowed balcony and plush redwood floors.

"Will you be able to get to school from this neighborhood? I mean, if you lived here—where are we heading—in the Castro district?"

Deborah nods and blows her nose. "I would take the M train."

"What train?" she asks. "We're on a MUNI bus, right? Or is this a streetcar? Have we been on a train?"

"No," Deborah says, though they took BART from the airport three days ago.

Her mother asks about BART, which she pronounces BARD. When Deborah doesn't answer, her mother asks again, leaning closer. Deborah remembers this routine from childhood—her mother's questions and her own nonresponse. When Deborah was ten, she spent a week walking around the house with a fake-fur hat pulled over her ears; when she was twelve she taped a sign to her forehead: NO TALKING ZONE. (Not that Deborah doesn't like to talk—before Selsa left she loved it. She just didn't want her own inner monologue interrupted.) Now, on the bus, when nothing comes out of Deborah's mouth, her mother glances at her. Deborah doesn't hide the tears streaming down her face—a common occurrence these days; they head straight for the creases in her nose.

"Oh," her mother says, and hands her a tissue from her other pocket, a fresh one.

The apartment in the Castro is a medieval-looking studio at the end of a long dark hallway. Black, thick bars block the side windows. Decals have been left on the panes: three snarling dog heads, Beware the Ogre, a horse with the head ripped off. Inside, the carpet, wine red heading toward maroon, smells lightless and airless, as if it has been cleaned with something hopelessly industrial. The paneled room is almost square, except one corner is missing. The corner apparently has been plastered in. Deborah doesn't even notice the anomaly until her mother says, "Isn't this an interesting shape?" She wanders around the room, holding her purse in both hands, looking but not really looking, in the way she has cultivated since Deborah has known her. Once, in the middle of a visit home from college, Deborah locked herself in the bathroom and cut her long straight hair into a ragged shag. Two days later, while watching television, her mother leaned forward in her chair and looked at her. "Oh, there's something different about your hair, isn't there?"

Now, in this cramped space with her mother, Deborah feels, suddenly, as if she is going to collapse. In her dissertation she writes about the vampirelike nature of grief in the early stages, but the extent of her sudden weakness still surprises her. She lies face down on the stiff carpet, her head resting on her hands. This is what she's come to, she thinks: a thirty-three-year-old woman who lies face down at her mother's feet. A month ago she was a woman who rolled up blueprints for architects all day and sat in seminars at night, a woman who couldn't take naps, who studied tap dancing on Sundays and danced circles around Selsa on their morning walk through the park. Deborah tries to think back to this other self, the one waving her arms, laughing so hard that food drops out of her mouth, the woman who lives underneath or perhaps just to one side of this sepulchral one.

She closes her eyes; fields of luminescent colors wash behind her lids: deep red, burnt orange, yellow, blue. The chemicals in her brain shift from gray to psychedelic, a dreamlike state. When she opens her eyes, she sees the flesh of her own thumb, and then she sees her mother's feet a few inches away, the beige toes of her walking shoes. When Deborah was a kid playing on the floor her mother would sit close by with the new baby in her lap and Deborah would stare at her mother's shoes, the same brand of orthopedic shoes

Heavier Than Air

she's wearing now, a half-inch heel, thick sides reinforced with a pad to support her fallen arches, which she passed on to Deborah.

Deborah puts her hand on her mother's foot and her mother pulls it away.

"Oh, you scared me," she laughs, taking a step back. She looks down at Deborah, bewildered for a moment. Then she slings her purse over one shoulder and folds her hands over her chest.

"Well," she says. "This isn't such a bad place. There's a big closet."

Deborah lifts her head high enough to see a brown door halfway open into what looks like a dark hole with concrete walls. There are gold bolts on the walls and on the ceiling. Deborah recognizes the bolts from S and M bondage photographs displayed at a bookstore in the Castro.

"Mom," she says. "That's not a closet, it's a dungeon." She lays her head back down: a dungeon may be all she can afford without Selsa.

"I suppose it's how you look at it," her mother says. She turns and walks down the hallway.

The first night Deborah's mother stayed in the apartment, she and Deborah watched a movie premiere on one of the main channels. Her mother sat on the couch and Deborah lay in an old nylon sleeping bag on the floor. Earlier, she had found a loose half-tab of Valium at the back of the bathroom drawer or it could have been a Vicodin leftover from Selsa's back injury. She was slightly woozy and numb. In the movie, a man paid someone to murder his wife to get money and start a new life in Arizona with his mistress. On the screen the blonde mistress was dumping drawers of papers onto the man's bed.

"Now, who is that character again?" her mother asked.

"The mistress," Deborah replied.

"What is she looking for, do you think?"

The woman tore through the man's closets, ripped open boxes, swept through the medicine cabinet.

"I don't know, Mom. She's probably looking for evidence so she can betray him."

"Oh," her mother said, disapproving and without a hint of irony, "people don't act like that."

When Deborah was a child, she would try to explain to her mother what was happening in movies. Her mother grew up without plumbing or electricity and saw her first movie, Gone with the Wind, at the age of twenty-four. But during her adolescence they got into horrible fights. "Mom, you're a champion card player, you've got a great memory," Deborah would shout. "Where the fuck does your mind go?" Her mother would cry and pull a crumpled tissue from her pocket; Deborah would stomp out of the room and feel guilty.

"People do act like that," she shouted now. "They act like that all the time." Then she buried her head in her sleeping bag. Through the nylon, she could hear her mother shift on the couch, and then she heard her stand up and walk into the kitchen. She expected to hear her crying, but when she came back she stood at Deborah's feet and sighed.

"Deborah," she began in a firm voice, as if she were about to deliver a speech she had practiced with her father before she got on the plane. "I know you are upset about Selsa. But I did not come here to be your whipping boy."

Later, after her mother had gone to sleep, Deborah lay in bed remembering Selsa and her mother arranging gifts under the tree one Christmas eve; Selsa wore her saffron-colored Sari with gold trim and her mother wore her brown robe and peach slippers. "That Selsa's a charmed girl," her mother had said. It was unusual for her to use the word charmed. When she heard that Selsa ran off with someone she said the same thing, "Oh, that's too bad. She was a charmed girl."

Deborah got out of bed and put on her shoes and went outside. The night was very dark and a coolness settled on her skin. She was sitting on the front steps of the apartment building looking up at the few visible stars when her neighbor who lived in the basement pulled up in her black Toyota truck.

"Hey," she said. "Are you okay?" She had a hairstyle like James Dean and her name was Shawn. One night about a month before Selsa left, Shawn had made them mushroom polenta and green beans. Selsa got so stoned she fell asleep on Shawn's bed and they had to hoist her up the stairs to Deborah and Selsa's apartment.

Deborah nodded. "My mother is visiting."

Shawn dug in her jeans pocket and offered Deborah a half-burned-out joint, which Deborah refused. "Parents are surreal," Shawn said. "My girlfriend's mom got hit by a car on the way to a Grateful Dead concert."

Deborah made a sympathetic noise—certainly she would rather have a live mother than a dead one.

"Yeah," Shawn continued. "A month before she was hit they were driving across Utah and her mom suddenly pulled over and stared up at something in the sky, and my girlfriend said, 'Mom,' she said, 'Why are you staring?' 'Oh, I don't know,' her mom said, 'the clouds were going so fast I just had to stop.' And then, you know, she was gone."

Deborah put her head in her hands. "Oh, that's so sad. I'm so sorry."

"Yeah," Shawn said. "Plenty sad."

The studio on Valencia and 27th is on the second floor. The wooden stairs wobble on their way up; her mother puts one hand on the wall.

"Oh, big," she says as they step into the room. It is the largest studio they have seen in two days of looking. The floors are gray painted wood. Two long windows look out on a blue building sporting white letters: ASP. Deborah can tell her mother wants to ask what the letters mean, why they are there. She feels sorry and relieved when instead her mother goes into the bathroom and flushes the toilet. Runs water into the sink. The kitchen is a separate room, or at least it is separated from the main room by a half wall. She opens and closes cupboards and turns on the stove: "Gas stove," she says out loud.

On the walk here, Deborah told her she couldn't answer more questions today. "Hm," her mother said, and stepped ahead of her to cross 24th Street.

A block later, her mother stopped at a window displaying a three-foot plaster wedding cake with plastic figurines on top, the kind Deborah imagines her mother had at her wedding.

"Nobody has cakes like that now," her mother announced. "Too old-fashioned." Deborah thought she sounded proud of her view, and maybe even contemptuous of the cake.

She had often wondered if her mother thought of her and Selsa as married. She's always had the impression that her mother liked thinking of her as her one grown single daughter, the first in generations, as far as Deborah knew. When Deborah was about to move to San Francisco with Selsa, her mother told her that she had once imagined herself single, working in a retail clothing shop for women in a city, and living in her own rented room with her own half-refrigerator and hot plate. She wouldn't mind using a bathroom down the hall. What her mother got was a flat-roofed three-bedroom house outside a small town. Wall-to-wall carpet. A husband. Eight children. A mudroom. Eventually a microwave. "That other life sounds lonely," Deborah had said, but her mother only shrugged and wiped a spot from her glasses.

Now, in the studio, Deborah stands a few feet from the windows in a sheet of light slanting between the buildings. The sunlight heats her scalp, making the roots of her hair tingle. Her mother has moved on from inspecting the kitchen and has decided to measure the main room. She places her feet carefully in a line, heel to toe. Deborah can hear her counting each footstep, out loud, under her breath. She can feel her passing one way, and then the other, as if her mother has a certain electrical charge specifically wired to the hair on Deborah's neck and the creases in her elbows.

"Twenty by fifteen," her mother says. She walks in a wide berth around Deborah but comes to stand at the windows directly in front of her. She shakes one window frame to see if it opens. It doesn't. She tries another. Up it goes and throws her off balance. Her mother's arms wave and her face distorts with panic for a moment. Deborah's arms fly out. She imagines her mother tumbling out over the sill. The bottoms of her beige shoes drop toward the concrete below.

Her mother catches herself.

"Golleeze," she breathes, patting her heart, "I didn't think that would happen."

Later, they are sitting at a café resting and drinking juice. Her mother pulls at the hem of her nylon socks. "You'd think they'd make socks that stay up, wouldn't you?" She looks at Deborah awaiting a response, but Deborah is listening to a sound inside her ears, Selsa's cooing laugh, and then another sound deep inside her, a whir, like the blades of a fan or windmill.

Her mother places her hand on Deborah's shoulder, then takes it away. "A person just wishes they could take some of that pain away from you," she says. Deborah lays her head on the table. Her mother takes a sip of her juice and stares into her cup. "Well," she says. And then "Well," again.

Six hours after Selsa drove off in her Honda Civic to the new woman's house, tears streaking her eyeliner and making her look like a madwoman in a Bollywood film, Deborah woke to a sharp pain like a cramp in her stomach. When the pain rode up to her esophagus she leaped out of bed and ran to the window for air. The next night she ran to the bathroom and vomited in the sink. When the pain arrived on the third night, she called her mother. As she moved toward the phone she could feel her body being taken over, a slow transfusion. She heard herself ask her mother to visit. She imagined lying in bed while her mother moved about the house; perhaps her mother would sit on the bed and hold her hand.

"You want me to come there?" her mother asked.

"Just for a week."

There was a long pause and whispering to her father, and then her mother's voice, loud and slightly excited.

This evening, her mother has agreed to cook for her. She sets a plate of food in front of her on the red and white-checkered tablecloth that Deborah bought in New York for Selsa on what they called their honeymoon, and then her mother stands there. Deborah doesn't know why.

"The meat patty got tough," her mother says. She has changed into her sleeping gear, a white nightgown that zips up the front like a robe. Peach slippers.

When she first arrived her mother said, "I'll clean, but I don't want to cook. I don't like to cook."

"You don't? I just thought we kids were too much for you."

"No, I never did. Your dad likes to cook more than I do."

The declaration explains differently the thousands of drab meals throughout Deborah's childhood. Tough meat straight up, never any spices or sauces. For spaghetti, she boiled noodles and put ketchup and butter on the table. When Deborah was eleven, or maybe ten, when Steven, the youngest, was born, her mother relinquished cooking the main meal altogether; Deborah remembers her in the kitchen in her brown housecoat. "I give up," she said, sticking an unwashed cereal bowl into the glasses cupboard. "You can just have grabs."

On the plate in front of Deborah is a beige piece of something, overcooked green beans, a slice of toast. She takes a bite of the

Heavier Than Air

beige—it must be ground chicken—when did her mother buy it? It's chewy, fairly tasteless, though she hasn't eaten chicken very often in the past ten years. Selsa did most of the cooking, spicy vegetarian Indian food, baby peas and corn steeped in hot red curry, chickpeas cooked with leeks in a creamy ginger sauce—Deborah would lick the curry and ginger from between Selsa's fingers. Now Deborah waits for saliva to gather in her mouth, to help her break the meat fibers down. Since Selsa left, she has mostly been ingesting Odwalla drinks: Super Protein, Mo' Beta, AntioxiDance. She can swallow, but chewing, the mechanisms of eating, seem unnatural: counter motion.

Her mother continues to stand next to the table until she has taken two bites. "Good," she says.

Deborah continues to chew and swallow. Halfway through, she puts the fork down. She hears her mother turn on the television, the rumble before she sets up the headphones. Deborah gets up and goes to her bedroom, sits at her desk in the walk-in closet and reads the last line of her dissertation: *As the adult child returns to the dead the acts of the living become like garish lamps disturbing the night.* Hogwash and mixed metaphors. She gets up and stands at the entrance to the living room. Her mother is slouched down on the couch, her feet on the coffee table, the remote control in her lap. At rest and in the dim light she looks twenty years younger than her seventy-one; her skin peachy and soft looking. She glances at Deborah and straightens a bit, makes a gesture like she'll turn on the volume. Shaking her head, Deborah sits on the other end of the couch and puts her feet on the coffee table. She closes her eyes and, in a moment, she hears her mother sink back into the couch and adjust herself on the pillows. She hears her mother sigh.

When Deborah was a kid, she and her mother watched *Days of Our Lives* and then *General Hospital.* Sometimes, during the school year, Deborah would fake sick so she could stay home and sit at her mother's feet, the latest baby napping in the pink room down the hall. One afternoon, after the shows were over, Deborah stood in front of the bathroom mirror forcing tears out of her eyes and whispering to some imagined suitor: *"Darling, I love you, I do. But I can never be with you."*

Her mother walked in with a stack of folded towels.

Deborah blushed. "I'm Laura Mathews."

Her mother shook her head and gave Deborah a strange look. "Oh, Deborah," she said, bending down to stuff the towels in the cupboard. "Don't be so dramatic."

Selsa had said this to her as well. After a fight, she would hold up her hands as if stopping traffic: "Deborah, please don't do the dramatics." But Deborah never imagined herself on the receiving end of Selsa's dramatics. It was as if Selsa had taken charge of the fantasy and discontinued Deborah's character, leaving her with no story, just theories of grief and a mother in her living room.

I have fallen in love with someone else and I can't stop it. I have to go.

The living room windows were dark and the clock in the kitchen ticked loudly. On the couch, Selsa held her arms tightly against her belly, her dark, bushy eyebrows and round cheeks impassive—it was a look Deborah had seen before but never directed at her. She put her hand on Selsa's knee—perhaps to reassure them both that everything would be all right, they could transcend anything that Selsa was about to say. But Selsa picked up Deborah's hand and placed it on the cushion between them. She looked Deborah straight in the face, stiff and resigned: *I have fallen in love with someone else. I can't stop it. I have to go.*

On the sixth day of her mother's visit, they take the N train into the Inner Sunset district. Cheaper rents. Fog. Her mother has never seen so many Asian people. "Do they speak English?" she asks.

"Some," Deborah says. "Probably most."

"Are they Chinese or Japanese?"

"Mostly Chinese," Deborah says. "And some Russians."

"The Russian language sounds like German," her mother says. Deborah's mother grew up speaking low German. She stopped speaking it because she felt ashamed. "It was a mistake not teaching you kids German," she says.

Deborah is walking fast. She slept for only a few hours, despair like sludge in her veins. Every time her mother asks her a question, she feels as if she is being hauled out of the ground, regression à la carte—she feels the way she sometimes felt living with her mother in a house full of kids, transparent within a diffused mix of homicide and suicide.

"Can we not talk for a while," she says. She tries to sound neutral, but her mother looks hurt. Her mouth makes an O, and then she looks away and clamps her lips together. A deep crease forms on her chin. Deborah is surprised—it's not a look she remembers from childhood. The look she most associates with her mother is smiling. She would smile down at her in their pew at church, her lips painted light orange or peach. The other look she remembers is from adolescence: confusion, fear. Sometimes tears. Once, when Deborah was fifteen, her mother told her she couldn't go to a lake party and Deborah said she would go anyway. "You've lost me," she said. "I'm already gone." Deborah moved out three weeks before she turned eighteen. She went home for family reunions and weddings.

The day is a bust as far as apartment hunting is concerned. The key from the rental agency doesn't work at the first place. The second place is an in-law requiring one to walk through the house of Mr. and Mrs. Chang. Mr. Chang lives in the living room with the television, which is far from the in-law apartment's entrance, but Mrs. Chang spreads out. Mrs. Chang follows Deborah around the apartment. Watches her face. Asks questions. For a moment, Mrs. Chang and Deborah's mother stand side by side, gazing at her inquisitively: the same round hairdo, the same round pleasant expressions.

Deborah cannot bear to see the third place. Her mother says they should take a quick look, but Deborah begins to march down Irving Street toward Tenth Avenue. Her mother scurries to keep up. She can hear her arms swing back and forth against her windbreaker. Deborah tries to slow down, but her mother waves her on: "Go. Go." She shoots down the sidewalk, turns up Tenth Avenue, barely stopping at red lights. She can see the green against blue of the park. She crosses Lincoln Street.

In the park, the air immediately softens. She hears birds. She hears plants, grass, trees.

But she doesn't hear her mother.

She turns and looks. Her mother is not there. She waits. Her mother doesn't arrive.

Deborah crosses back over Lincoln and begins to retrace her steps.

"Mom," she calls out. A few people look at her. "Mother!"

Deborah walks back into the park and then back out of the park, all the way to the street where she last noticed the swishing windbreaker. Her mother is nowhere. For a moment Deborah panics, she can smell something burning. No. Eucalyptus and lilacs. A soft blue light emanates from the lilac bushes. Her breathing softens. No mother. No questions. She walks back into the park and wanders into the middle of a green square and sits under a tree facing the road. She closes her eyes. An ant crawls over her arm and she can feel it travel between the hairs and across her elbow.

If there is no mother perhaps there is no daughter.

She thinks this is what it might feel like to be free—she has read articles about people who suddenly step out of their lives into a free-falling state of complete detachment.

A tall woman is pushing a stroller toward Deborah on the paved path. Her baby is kicking the footrest repeatedly. Deborah thinks about asking the woman if she has seen her mother, but only breath exits her mouth.

She leans further into the tree and looks up through its leaves at the deepening blue sky. The air is turning cool with evening. In the orange threads of the leftover sun she catches a glimpse of something new, an open prairie, a vastness, an ocean of fog rolling down from the hills. She feels cut loose in a way she has not felt for a long time, perhaps ever. Mother. Behind her lids, she sees her mother's inquisitive face, open and round. And even when her mother's face appears distorted by fear, hazel eyes clouded, Deborah's chest continues to expand until she must tilt her own face toward the sky, a bowl of dark blue, the darkest and most beautiful of blues, her mother wandering under this same beauty, in the darkness of the park.

She can feel someone sit beside her. A rustling of windbreaker and then silence. They sit for a long while breathing in silence, until Deborah's mother whispers, "My butt is getting wet," and for a moment Deborah's face is smiling so widely the bones of her cheeks feel as if they will stretch out like wings and carry her away.

On the walk home Deborah asks her mother to tell a story about her mother's childhood on the farm. She looks nervous for a moment. "I mean, what did you like to do as a kid?" Deborah asks. She thinks her mother will tell her about feeding calves from a bottle, or about canning tomatoes. Her mother tips her head and squints at the sky. "Well, I used to like to chomp gophers," she says.

"Chomp gophers?" Deborah asks, and her mother stops and demonstrates by pretending she has a stick in her hand. "My brother Alquin would pour water down the hole and then the gophers came up the other hole," she says. She brings her stick down on the sidewalk.

"You mean you killed them?" Deborah finds it difficult to imagine her mother, who couldn't even swat their dogs, chomping repeatedly into the head of a gopher.

"They ate the crops and we didn't have enough traps," she says, shrugging and frowning at her as if she were being foolish. "You do what you have to do, Deborah. Everyone knows that."

The next day on their way into the building from grocery shopping they run into Shawn, who bows and calls her mother "Mrs. Mother," which her mother likes. "So, you're the mother," Shawn says, and takes her mother's hand and kisses her fingers, which to Deborah's surprise makes her mother blush. On their way up the stairs her mother says, "Now that's a nice young man," and Deborah doesn't bother to correct her.

There is a note on the door from Selsa. As soon as Deborah sees Selsa's handwriting, her brain starts to shhhhh with the static of everything she longs to hear: *I made a mistake. I still love you.*

Selsa forgot to take her silverware.

The silverware drawer has crumbs in it, a few grains of basmati rice. There is a spoon with a Yogi Bear–shaped handle that Deborah gave to Selsa two birthdays ago. She puts it into a plastic bag. There are forks from India that Selsa's mother passed on to her, some knives, spoons. At the last minute she folds up the tablecloth and puts that in the bag too.

"I'm going up the hill," Deborah tells her mother, who has been watching her. Selsa has an office up the hill at the Jesuit university. Her mother knows this. She puts her shoes back on and is waiting at the door. "You don't have to come with me," Deborah says, but her mother follows her into the hall. They trudge silently up the hill and up the stairs past the Saint Ignatius church her mother attends every morning. Her mother's lips are moving and Deborah suspects she is saying a silent rosary. She follows Deborah across the campus lawn and into the chemistry building and up the four flights of stairs. The building is empty. Deborah sets the plastic bag full of silverware outside Selsa's door. She can smell sage and saffron and lemon—Selsa's smell. Should you leave a note? her mother asks. But what could Deborah possibly say? *I'll give you anything you want, come back.*

Deborah shakes her head.

On the way home, Deborah suddenly stops and sits on the stairs leading up from Fulton Street. Her mother sits down beside her. The wind has grown cool, and Deborah can feel the evening fog drifting in from the ocean. Tomorrow will be gray and cold and wet.

"Mom, do you ever wish you'd had a different life, I mean without children?" she asks.

For a moment, Deborah thinks her mother is going to ignore the question. She suspects her mother would have chosen a different life. She blinks and looks down at the steps, confused. But then her mother raises her head and looks at her.

"No, I really don't," she says. "Not anymore."

Later, after Deborah washes her face and takes a bath, her mother takes out photographs she brought from Minnesota, family pictures at Deborah's fifth, tenth, and twelfth birthdays. Bleached-out hair, green green grass. None from adolescence. They sit on the couch and her mother points Deborah out to herself.

"You were a happy child."

"How did you know?" Deborah asks. "Anyone can smile for a picture."

"No, you were happy. You would put on that flouncy dress I made for you girls and twirl in the driveway."

Deborah remembers that dress: dark blue printed with red and yellow flowers. White rickrack on the hem. For a moment, she sees a flash of white, a wavy white line blurring across her vision. In some of the photographs, her mouth is caught wide open and her cheeks are fat and round.

That night, Deborah wakes up to the pain again. She climbs out of bed and makes her way through the dark to the living room. Her mother is lying on her back with one arm draped over her face. Deborah climbs onto the bed and tugs on her mother's shoulder. *Mom*, she whispers. Her mother lifts her head from the pillow, her hazel eyes look black. She reaches out her hand, and then her eyes roll back and her lids close and her head falls back to the pillow. A swath of her brown hair sticks to her pale forehead.

The room is getting darker—but Deborah can see the luminous white of her mother's nightgown, her pale skin. She lies next to her, puts her hand on her mother's hip. The tip of her nose brushes against her mother's hair.

In the morning, Deborah wakes in her own bed to the sound of her mother on the phone making plane arrangements with Deborah's father. "Dad," she says, "do you know what ASP means?"

Tomorrow, early, her mother leaves for Minnesota; today, after her mother visits Saint Ignatius, they are going to Glen Park to see a small one-bedroom sunny with view, and then to Dolores Park to see a studio with bay windows.

Deborah hears the apartment door open and close. She jumps out of bed, hurries to dress.

The morning air chills her neck; she was right about the fog.

The church feels like a cave; the light is dim and the sound of the few people praying diffuses around her ears and then travels up into the high domed ceiling: the prayers her mother spoke when Deborah was in her womb, the rhythm in her bones and muscles. Deborah kneels three rows behind her mother at an angle that makes her mother's profile visible. Her mother's eyes are closed, light brown eyelashes resting on her lower lids, praying for all of her children, and for Deborah her fourth daughter, who sang and stood on her head for visitors, who would laugh so hard at the kitchen table she'd choke.

Later, on the bus, her mother stares out at the city streets. Deborah can see the fine hairs covering her peach-colored skin, the skin

Heavier Than Air

she passed on to Deborah, and she can see the wrinkles around her eyes and the tan age spots on her neck and collarbone. She leans her head against her mother's shoulder and her mother pats her arm. Her shoulder is soft; she smells like Minnesota air. Outside, the sun is beaming on the concrete sidewalks. She sees her mother's face reflected in the bus window, squinting at the skyline. And then suddenly the wind blows up a piece of paper, and her mother startles. Deborah sees her mother's younger face at their kitchen window, half blurred by the glass, and Deborah in the gravel driveway, twirling and laughing, her wheat-blonde hair flying out like streaks of sunlight.

The Fifth Season

"DO YOU remember when all the neighborhood kids had ring-worm?" he asked me from his hospital bed, inviting me to imagine, I suppose, that the lesions corrupting his brain were a similar phenomenon. I said yes, but really only one kid in the neighborhood had had ringworm, and it wasn't even ringworm—it was impetigo. Or so I remember.

"Come lie in the bed with me," he said. He said it every time I went to visit him. There was a large window near his bed. Out the window I see gray—perhaps the roof of another building or it could be that the sky was gray every time I went there. The room was on the fourth floor. It was winter. In the beginning it was winter, and then at the end it was spring. But all I see is gray, very continuous, something to count on. I think there was another man in the room, near the door. There was another man, and then later there was not another man. He is gray as well, but shadowy, off to the side.

Marc pulled back the sheet and blanket and patted the space beside him. The bed was narrow, like all hospital beds, but I climbed into that space and lay on my back with my legs straight ahead of me, my arms pressed to my sides—it was what I could do. We would pretend we were still children; or we would slip into that late-eighties, early-nineties script that had enamored Hollywood and the American public: *Philadelphia, Early Frost, Long Time Companion*— gay man dying, loyal friends hold his hand to the dirty end. I felt under the sheets for his hand. There. Warm and muscular, surprisingly life driven. He was dying from the neck up, the rest of his body uncorrupted, muscled, blood fed. I looked ahead of me at the wall—there was something on the wall, a card or a painting, blue—and I held his hand.

His left eyelid was collapsing. An inelegant drooping into the corner as if gravity were exerting unfair pressure. At first the drooping had given him a lazy, sexy look, but now the skin cloaked more and more of his eye each time I went. His eyes were brown. I didn't go often enough. The small bones inside both his ears were closing in tightly to his eardrums. Nerves shut off, the auditory system smothered. By the time he was admitted into San Francisco General he was stone deaf, but he could read lips and we had a clipboard we passed back and forth. Yellow paper with blue lines.

"Do you want some hot chocolate?" he whispered to me. We had often on winter days as kids, after destroying the snow in our backyards, sipped hot chocolate on stools in his mother's kitchen: dark green cupboards, a photograph of a Oaxacan market on the wall. But the whispering annoyed me, and I was embarrassed that it annoyed me. It was desperate, not childlike but childish—though I don't remember him talking like that as a child.

"Take some money from my bag and go downstairs and get yourself hot chocolate."

"I don't want any hot chocolate," I said.

"You don't want any?" he asked, turning further on his side to see my lips and watch my face.

"No."

"Is something wrong?"

"No, I just don't need any hot chocolate." I had taken money from his bag the week earlier and had returned with two cardboard cups of hot chocolate from a machine in the basement cafeteria. Instant, watery, sweet. A distraction.

A nurse came in with a blood pressure hose over his neck. He had red hair, diluted by sun or bleach. "Don't get up," he said, gently, "I'll come back." I'd watched him take Marc's pulse the week before; how did he keep his fingernails so clean?

"No, it's all right, I've got to go," I said. I'd been there for over an hour; he slept and then woke; we talked with the yellow pad about the lesions and the possibility of cutting them out with laser technology. But the lesions would just grow back, like thistles.

"What?" Marc asked. He put his hand on my arm and looked up into my face.

"I've got to go," I repeated, slowly, more slowly than necessary. "T h e   n u r s e   i s   h e r e ."

The nurse stepped to the foot of the bed and turned his head politely—or to spare himself the awkward deceit.

Marc moved his hand up my arm and sat forward, bringing his eyes to me, pulling me down toward him until our foreheads were an inch apart. I couldn't recall being this physically close since first grade, yet something seemed familiar. A violence. I could see the clear mucus gathering in the corner of the drooping eyelid and the completely unmasked plea in the other. Dark brown. Lighter now than when he was a kid. I could have been there only thirty minutes. Fear and fearlessness. Nothing to lose. Emptiness and grasping. A golden ring around the pupil.

"Hot chocolate?" he asked, his lips not closing around the words as they came from the back of his throat and rode out on his breath. They sounded like "ha chohtlate." He pointed down, toward the cafeteria. I covered my mouth to suppress a laugh and looked away.

A blue print on the wall, blue and yellow and some milky white and I want to say the image was a horse, a print of that famous yellow horse, and that his mother, who had flown in from Minnesota the week before and was staying with his sister Lynn in Richmond, taped the poster there, but I don't think that's true. I don't know how that print got on that wall, though it is true that Marc loved paintings and prints and when he lived in London and New York visited the galleries regularly and when he came back talked about the art incessantly. But Marc had nothing for horses; I am the one who in shorts and T-shirt rode a Shetland around our backyard and into the cornfield behind our houses one summer, until the horse bucked me off and my forearm snapped in two places, and then for the rest of the summer into the school year Marc carried things around for me. A biology book. My coronet on band days. An empty black plastic purse.

The nurse was wearing a white T-shirt and white pants—of course he was. I smiled. Marc could see my lips—I wore lipstick all the time then. "Yes," I said. "Hot chocolate in the cafeteria."

And then I'd be gone, walking quickly past the other man in the bed by the door and turning into the brightness and anonymity of the hallway.

Marc Randolf Nesserich, later known as Marc Wendell Britain. I think I was the only person in San Francisco who knew he wasn't upper-class Protestant: his grandmother was Mexican, his mother and Aunt Zola vacationed with Mexican cardinals and priests. His father, German-American Catholic like the rest of the town, had been a low-level manager at the Melrose Electrical Cooperative. He would have earned little more than the other men in the neighborhood, who labored at the Kraft and Jenny-O Turkey Plants, if he hadn't over twenty years embezzled more than a hundred grand of community profit.

The day the embezzlement news broke in the *Melrose Daily*, Marc wasn't on the bus or in school. He wasn't on the bus the next day, or

Heavier Than Air

the next, or the next. I spied him one late afternoon through the evergreens in our backyard; he was wandering around shirtless in a light snowfall, his ill-defined, hairless golden chest flecked with snow. He might have been my first conscious experience of human beauty. Another day I heard him singing Spanish songs and knocking around a golf ball, though he hated golf. And then one day the Nesseriches' house was empty, driveway and backyard barren. Marc visited the neighborhood only once during my high school years, and I was at swim practice.

"What an odd boy," women in the neighborhood often said.

"He's even weirder than you," said my brothers.

But that was later, wasn't it? Wasn't he first just a really sweet kid with dark gold skin, a large head and narrow shoulders?

I can see him out our bathroom window sitting on the swing set in our backyard. He was five, or maybe six. He sat there and waited for me to come out and play with him: barefoot, one toe pushing the swing off from the ground just enough to make motion. He wasn't swinging as much as swaying. The swing swayed and wobbled and he looped one arm around the chain and with his free hand picked at his mosquito bites or the hem of his shorts. He could wait a long time, sometimes until his mother hollered out their back door, and then she'd holler again and he'd look up at the bathroom window as if he knew I was there or had been there. He'd push himself off the swing and slowly make his way across our yard, careful to step around my father's carrot and onion garden, and through the shadows of the evergreens, where he'd disappear.

"Marc!" I called out to him through the window screen. It was June and I could feel the heat from outside move through the tiny screen holes onto my face. He looked up from his swing and waved—his eyes were rounder than other people's eyes.

"Are you coming outside?"

"Maybe. I ate lunch."

"Come out and play."

"Maybe. It's hot."

"The hose," he said and pointed.

My father's garden hose snaked around behind the house and we had on occasion pelted ourselves with water. The water came directly from a ground well that my father dug in our backyard; it was cold, a wild cold, the kind that moves through the skin to the veins immediately and confuses the blood. Spanking cold, my father would say. I stepped down from my stool by the window and a minute later appeared at our back garage door and then ran at him on the swing as if I were going to tackle him. But he didn't scare; he grinned and lifted his shoulders and stuck his chin out in delight. I captured him and pulled him to his feet. I dragged him a yard or two, marveling at his limpness and lightness, how he could allow his body to be taken over, how he would give it to me.

"Stand up," I said, and then he did that too. He was a few inches shorter than I was, though later half a foot taller, and he was scrawnier, less muscled, less self-possessed. I loved him. Once I squeezed his forearm so fiercely that a bright indigo bruise rose up the length of it—like a miracle—and I told him to run home and tell his mother he fell from the swing. Another time, in the middle of a ground blizzard, I made him walk behind me through the town and around the S-curve to home. No talking, no touching my shadow on the snow.

Some things he wouldn't do: he refused to eat our dog's poop. Another time I dug a hole in the garden—before my father had planted—and put Marc in the hole, but he wouldn't let me bury him. I got as far as covering his legs, arms and torso to his upper chest—not even to his neck—and he popped up suddenly, shaking the half-frozen black loamy dirt off his shirt and pants, and wiping off his knees and elbows.

At the beginning of that summer, Marc had knocked at our side door: "Do you want to come to my birthday party?" he asked. I said sure and then he took me by the hand and walked me through the neighbor's backyard and to the back of his house. His yard was browning, needed water, a large expanse of browning grass that led up to the two concrete steps that led into his garage that led into his one-story house. Charcoal gray, the darkest house in the eight-house neighborhood. And dark inside as well. A palpable thickness shrouded his house, as though his father's embezzling had been spinning an aura, a murky tension the color of river water. Marc's mother and father stood ahead of us in the dark hallway, two faceless unformed blobs. No one else was home.

"Who is this sweet little girl?" his father bent at the knees, his belly hanging down between them like a full sac. I was supposed to move forward. I stood still. Marc took my hand—so small. Slightly sweaty but clean feeling. There we are in the dark hallway, the top of his large head at my cheekbone, my fine white hair chopped off under my ears, or above my ears.

"Is this your girlfriend?" his father asked. His mother laughed. "She's his wife," she said. "Lorrie, you're going to marry Marc, aren't you? You're going to be Marc's wife, huh?"

On the table, red party hats and a blazing eight-inch double-layered chocolate cake—yet I was the only guest at the party. Was I the only one invited? Would no one else come? I strapped a hat on Marc's large head, and then one on mine, but the emptiness kept coming and made me pull him closer—his wrist bones settling next to mine. A delicate sharpness. The hat string cut into the baby fat on my neck.

Husband. Wife. One dark, one light. One graduating from Melrose High School and then flailing around the country in old thrift-store slips and hiking boots until landing in the Western Addition in San Francisco. One fag, one dyke. Postcards. Telephone calls. Two visits. One disappearing for five years, traveling to Mexico, London, New York, answering phones in Soho and memorizing museum plaques. And then suddenly reappearing, on a Sunday afternoon on his old friend's Page Street painted-black doorstep, a nickel-sized Kaposi's lesion passing as a nothing, a birthmark on the tender side of his elbow inside his sleeve.

Toxoplasma gondii. Marc taught me this word. A common parasite in cats, crescent shaped, ghostly. This was just months before protease inhibitors. On a postmortem photograph, the parasites looked like fingernail clippings with an eye. Or like sperm without a tail. Floaty, harmless-looking debris that infiltrates the immuno-logically hijacked blood, travels to the brain, destroys the neuron insulation and instigates the overproduction of mysterious white matter. A cross section of Marc's left hemisphere showed a dense network of delicate, wavy branches webbed with snow.

He wrote "help me" on the blue-lined pad.

"What do you mean 'help me'?" I asked.

He wrote the words bigger.

H E L P   M E.

I changed the subject. "Do you remember when everyone went down to the river on Christmas Eve and took off their clothes?" I wrote. Actually, I had turned back from the river out of fear, and when I got home I had told my parents what the kids were doing and they had told Marc's parents. There he is, a ten-year-old boy being hauled up over the bank toward the snowy field by his arm, his mother screaming at him in Spanish and swatting his bare backside and legs.

Marc took hold of my wrist and brought his eyes to mine—a tinge, a memory but not quite.

"Do you need to say something to me?" he whispered.

And just then, for the first time in at least ten years, I remembered. And he knew I remembered. Not the river scene, but three years later. The beginning of eighth grade, months before his father was busted and he and his family disappeared. I was supposed to be at lunch in the cafeteria, but I was breaking rules, wandering on my own schedule. I decided to go into the art supply room to get something. A certain type of paper. The art room was dark. Everything was lumps, the long wooden tables, the dismal clay sculptures of the previous class. I stepped through the classroom into the back supply room. Past an abandoned stack of something, maybe chairs, half covered with a black tarp. I saw boxes farther back. I dropped to my knees and started feeling around with my hands. The smell of boxes and paper and glue.

I didn't know he was in the room, though we had on occasion hid out there, or at least I didn't know it all the way. And then something landed on my back, collapsing me into a box, and I felt his hand fumbling at the front of my shirt. He had grown so much bigger than me. His mouth was in my hair and it felt like he was tearing strands out with his teeth—that's how it felt. Was he kissing me? Like he was finding individual strands and yanking them out. His hands were tearing at the buttons of my shirt, one hand pushing down the shirt into my bra.

I didn't yell. Maybe I didn't want him punished, or I was preserving something, my own reputation—not for sex but for truancy and general misbehavior—already shot. I didn't speak his name. A button jettisoned onto the concrete and pinged, another fell into my mouth. I spit out the button and then I reached up behind me with one arm and drilled my fingernail, the one I kept long for prying open tabs on pop cans, into his fleshy midriff. But the fingernail wasn't what stopped him—was it? A noise, someone came into the art room, the teacher. And then Marc was gone.

I lay for a moment, cheek on the concrete. The cold feels good even now. It could have been a dare. Or payback. Or maybe he just couldn't stand to be alone in his own body anymore. I didn't speak to him for the rest of the school year—what would we say? I still don't know where to put it.

From his hospital bed, Marc continued to look at me. That eye. Immaculate, manipulative, fading into gold now, the pupil shot through with fear and a low, continuous dose of morphine in his saline. His white hospital gown tangled at his waist, exposing a bare hip. Marc's energy, his eyes, his skin, his gestures were returning to the beauty and barbarism of nature. A wilderness radiated from him. Sometimes I felt as if a freshly killed deer were splayed in the middle of the room, its spirit loosened, bragging, obscene, its neck thrown back in morbid ecstasy.

"No," I said, staring blankly back at him. How dare he, I thought. He was blown open, but I had to keep on going, didn't I? Death waiting around, posing as a fifth season.

"Please, stop looking," I said, and he obediently turned his gaze to the wall.

The yellow horse was galloping across the blue. Not galloping, flying, its muscles shot through with flight. The possibility—that's what the painter was after. The exuberance of the yellow, the defiance of a flying horse, the imagination hurling past reason. On that same wall was something else—a crucifix? Yes, there must have been a crucifix in that room, but not on that wall. Above the bed: a black crucifix with a white figure nailed to the wood; his mother would have put that there as well. I can see the folds of Jesus' skirt, his sorrowful European neck, the resigned, released posture. I can see the long slim fingers hanging over the edge of the wood, beautifully carved, translucent.

I looked down at the pad. H E L P M E. He could never stay in the lines.

"But I want you to help me," I wrote, and handed it to him.

He looked excited with one eye. "How?" he said. "How can I help you?"

"I need advice," I said. "This woman has been following me around in her truck. Last week on my walk home from the hospital she rolled down the window and asked me for a date. It would just be sex," I said. Was already sex, every night in the front seat of her truck, parked outside my apartment building, her tattooed carpenter's hand teasing my underwear, pulling the lip down and playfully slapping my bottom.

Marc took the pad from me. "Don't see her," he wrote.

"Why?" I asked. "You've had plenty of sex dates."

He took the pad again. "Look where I am," he wrote. And then he wrote, "You don't know the difference between sex and love."

I read the note and laughed, but he was wrong. I did know the difference, but for now it didn't matter.

"You promised me you wouldn't die for another year," I had written the week before.

"You think I'm dying? I'm not dying," he said, suddenly straight and indignant. He made an extraordinary face, considering the drooping eyelid; he pressed his nose into the air toward the yellow horse, as if he were pressing into a new reality, and then he lay back down, curled on his side, and fell asleep.

"Don't see her," he whispered again now. I promised him I wouldn't but was already sprawled across her big lap, sex a kind of temporary transcendence. His drooping eyelid collapsed completely, dragging the other lid down with it. He lay on his back and held up his hand. I was supposed to take it; he hated falling asleep alone. He had always hated being alone—instead of sitting in his basement room listening to KWOL like the rest of us seventh graders, Marc traipsed around behind a posse of older neighborhood boys, who predictably taunted him and cuffed him on the shoulder or the back of his head.

I set the pad on the hospital table at the head of the bed and stood looking at him for a while. He still wore one ring on his middle finger—it reminded me of a bishop's ring, though I've never seen one. I took his hand. A shadow behind me. His sister. Usually when I was there, she would go to the cafeteria, or hang in the hallway just outside the door. Death duty.

She looked sad. Did I look sad? He was supposed to die weeks ago. Her eyes were round and brown like his. Long eyelashes, thick wavy black hair trailing down to chubby hips. She was a nurse, an RN somewhere in Richmond.

"I wish he would just let go." Lines delivered to me two weeks earlier—and only now do I forgive her.

I pictured Marc on a rope in midair. He had swung on a gymnastics rope through the gymnasium in the middle of a school lecture. About a month before his father was indicted. Mr. Ricklick pulled him down, dragged him up the aisles by his hair.

He's a twenty-nine-year-old man, I thought. Why should he let go?

"Except for the eye, he looks good, doesn't he," she said now. "He would like to look good when he dies."

"Yes," I said. "He looks like a healthy young man."

What is there to say, what can sisters, mothers, lovers, friends say? He was alive and then he was dead, like so many others. Narration only makes him more dead—as we march up and down Market Street in our orange lace bustiers and leather chaps. As we swallow our cocktails and eat tuna sandwiches on the steps of City Hall in tuxedos and wedding gowns. But I have photographs. Age four on his clean-cut front lawn, shrouded in the black and white dress of a Franciscan nun, his sweet round eyes and pudgy face in the habit, devout, beseeching. Age ten on the school bus, thick wavy brown hair eclipsing his ears, his wool poncho—a prize from Mexico City—swinging around his knees. In his mid-twenties, cross-legged on my black-painted steps, imitating (for me?) the bored look of Elvis Presley, whom he didn't respect, paging through an Encyclopedia Britannica, a text he did respect.

There. On the telephone. Three months before the hospital, the late-autumn sun falling onto my bare feet through the bay windows of my small living room, a finger over my free ear so I can hear him.

"Marc? Marc is this you?"

Heavier Than Air

He was weeping.

"I don't know where I am," he said.

He was in Minneapolis for Thanksgiving, visiting his mother and sisters. He'd had an ear infection for six weeks before he left.

"What do you mean, you don't know where you are? Where is your mother?"

I can hear him breathing into the phone, and I can hear the static sound of a public space.

"I don't know. We're in a mall. I'm dizzy, I lose my balance."

"You're in a mall," I repeated. "They took you to a mall and now where are they?"

"I think they're trying on dresses. I don't know."

"They're trying on dresses. And they left you alone?"

He got suddenly very quiet. "Yes," he whispered dramatically. This was when the whispering began. "Lorrie, I'm alone."

"No, you're not alone," I said. "Forget that. We'll just stay on the phone until you see them again. Now, get a bench and sit down."

I heard him moving and the shifting of the telephone cord.

"I'm sitting," he said. "A lady wants to use the phone."

"She can't. Now tell me about your trip, are they being nice to you?"

He and Bernie, his mother, had visited the old neighborhood, he told me. It was snowing; the kind of light November snow that floats down like pieces of white ash. The snow was three inches deep on the backyard, undestroyed. "Where are the children?" he kept asking me. "We are the children," I told him. Bernie had taken him for a walk through the yards, but he became frightened of the ice under the snow and he kept falling and she yelled at him.

"I can't hear out of my right ear," he said to me.

"You can't hear anything in one ear?"

Static again and then a new silence. When I was nineteen, I had lived alone for six months in a hollow outside Pyatt, Arkansas. I slept in a mud-floor shack some hippies had left behind; the shack was a mile into the hollow, three miles from the nearest gravel road and ten miles from the nearest house. At night I lay under sleeping bags and furs and stared into the dense darkness, the grandest darkness I've ever seen, darkness that doesn't end at your skin but infiltrates your cells, and thickens, and begins to make sounds.

"Bernie doesn't understand," he said. "I'm dying."

And I knew he needed to hear me say what I really thought. "Yes," I said. "You are starting to die."

A long breath, as though he were breathing the words in. And then another long silence that wasn't really silence. I can barely hear the words when he says them.

"I haven't done anything important yet and now I'm going to degrade myself," he says. "Oh, god, it makes me feel sick—Lorrie, you're not going to write about it, are you?"

And the phone went dead.

This day isn't gray. This day cracks open with some pale blue. Marc's eyelids are closed, in each corner a crusted pool of blood. His face is like a placid lake. I reach under the covers and find his hand: amazingly cold. Spanking cold. Heavy the way a dead cat is heavy. I try to bend his fingers but they pop back up into straight position.

I wait for him to lift his hand. I wait for him to open his one eye and pat the windowless side of the bed. I hold up a photograph I brought with me that morning: he and I lying head to head on the gray carpet in my Dolores Street apartment, staring up directly into the camera. He is confident. Smiling. Legs crossed at the ankles.

An hour earlier, before his mother and sister had gone home for the afternoon to return in the evening, his sister had given me a small brown bottle of liquid opium. "Just a drop or two on his tongue, just if he gets in too much pain," she had said, her brown eyes wet, rims swollen. I sat in the plastic chair and stared at him. The other man in the room was already gone. The bed empty.

Heavier Than Air

I turned the bottle over in my palm.

The day before, I had walked into the room and Marc was urinating in the corner by the windows. The IV and oxygen tubing splayed across the floor, white sheets speckled beautifully with red. "Marc, go back to bed," I ordered, but he flung his arms against the wall; he started pounding, howling, no sign of morphine in his eye. The red-haired nurse and two orderlies rushed in and pinned his arms to his sides, pushed him toward the floor or maybe it was the bed. "Don't do that to him," I yelled, and began to cry and then for the first time I couldn't stop crying. The red-haired nurse turned to face me and he said what he had to say. "Visitors must leave the room."

The night before Marc died, I lay on the floor of my small apartment and cranked up the volume on the stereo—but I could still hear the pounding of my angry sobs against my throat. I had turned the carpenter away. The sun went down and the room went black, and then suddenly I raised my feet and kicked the wall beneath the window; I kicked and kicked until the plaster gave way and a fine white dust powdered the floor. It was an exquisite feeling; I imagine even now the thudding in my feet and ankles like buffalo stampeding, and I wanted to break everything, to bellow Fuck you, you don't understand you stupid stupid people. Finally, the neighbors knocked on my door, and I stopped, and my breath calmed, and I heard through the open window the wild renegade parrots of San Francisco, escaped from their cages and living in the palm trees on Dolores Street, screeching at the top of their lungs.

Husband. Wife. One dark, one light. One sitting in a sunny window on Steiner Street twelve years later, and one scattered into the Northern Hemisphere, dissipated molecules, the final diaspora.

And in the backyard, one turning on the hose and chasing the other with water. One screaming and throwing his chest forward, his ribs ecstatic and arching toward the sun and the skin of his round golden belly gleaming as his shorts and underwear slide down and catch on his hips. She swings the hose wildly around her head, like a lasso, and he gallops in a narrow circle, until the end of the hose predictably smacks the back of his head. The water turns pink there—a sudden pink froth—and his screaming shifts tone as he runs to get away from whatever is hurting the back of his head: a darker C minor chord, a frightened painful bawling.

"Stop!" I shout. He stops.

"Sit down." He sits on the grass in front of me. I can see the back of his head where I part his dark hair. A crooked pink gash. A slit in the back of his head, oozing red onto my fingertips. If I could open the gash and look inside, I would see the human brain, a wormy timeless mass undulating with thoughts, feelings, memories—and the infestation, our greed, our fear.

I would see a mass of gray. A rooftop. Wavy branches webbed with snow.

"There there," I said, "it's nothing." I must have heard the phrase on television, or it was something my mother said. He calmed, and I patted the slightly sticky, wet hair into place, and leaned forward and kissed the back of his head.

"Am I going to be all right?" he asked.

"Yes," I answered confidently. "You're going to be just fine."

Heavier Than Air

THE CASKET was shining white, and my mother wore a cotton white dress with small clear buttons and nothing around the neck, nothing on her face or wrists or fingers, except her thin gold wedding band.

"She'll go up to the Lord like a helium balloon," Dee said.

I stood next to Dee, feeling the weight of my legs and breathing into the tops of my lungs. I couldn't stop watching my mother's face, looking for a sign, something. My mother was sixty-five years old, but her face had been made round and smooth. She looked like a woman who had never had three children. I knew my mother was going into the ground, yet I too imagined her floating up into the arms of Jesus. A nonbeliever, I still hoped this. My mother had spent the last twenty years, since I was nine and Dee was fifteen, praising the Lord in a convalescent home for the mentally ill. My father likes to say she was a woman who lived for her soul and nothing else.

Cheryl, the middle sister who ran a grocery in Greenwald, sat in the front row of metal chairs. Her cream-colored blouse hung a size too big over her shoulders and I couldn't help thinking that she looked like she had as a child, before our mother left—that we all did. Even Dee with her gaunt face and tailored suit was leaning back on one hip like she had at fifteen. We were three grown daughters, none of us mothers. We all kept looking at the woman in the casket, waiting for her to sit up and see that we were there, waiting for her to speak.

Except for two members of my father's ex-congregation who remembered my mother from her young evangelist days, the rest of the wake room was empty. Still, my father whispered as if he didn't want to disturb anyone. He wore the same black suit he had worn in my childhood to preach and baptize and marry people. The fabric was worn across the chest from hugging. For a moment, I wanted to tell him about my pregnancy, the six-week-old fetus wreaking havoc with my digestive system. He put his hand lightly on my shoulder, reassuringly, the way he had when I was a girl standing next to him greeting people at the back of the church.

"She was a trouper," he said.

Dee convulsed forward, laughing. I excused myself and ran to the bathroom.

On the plane going home, Dee's helium balloon line came back to me and I laughed. Dee didn't even know my story.

In the summer of 1975, my mother drove all over Church Grove County, a predominantly Catholic community, delivering the Lord's message in pamphlets. A week after my ninth birthday, two months before she went into the home, she took me along and we saw a work crew setting up canvas tents for a county fair in an unplanted wheat field. I asked if we could go to the fair, but she just stared out the window at the road. I didn't think she heard me, and I tugged on her sleeve. Then, about two miles past the fair my mother suddenly pulled the car over onto the shoulder and we got

Heavier Than Air

out. She took my hand and we walked the two miles back down the dirt road. I was wearing my pointed little patent leather shoes and no hat under the hot sun.

Dee would say Mother stopped the car out of anger or punishment, but I don't believe that is entirely true. My mother liked to walk long distances in any direction and I don't think it ever occurred to her that two miles there and back would be painful for me. My mother didn't think like that. She saw herself as my teacher, but she also saw us as buddies or equals. She was just driving along listening to the hum of the Minnesota heat and the Lord told her to stop.

At the fair site stood two red canvas tents and a few game booths. When we reached the first booth, my mother bought me a big clear balloon and tied it to my finger. On the way back to the car she held my hand and the balloon tugged at the other. I curled my finger and held my arm above my head. The string on my finger pulled tighter and cut off the blood.

"The balloon hurts my finger," I said.

My mother stopped walking and looked at me as if she'd just remembered I was there. She was wearing heels and a yellow dress with a white collar. Looking very thoughtful and stooping next to me, she carefully examined my finger where the string was tied. She followed the string up to the balloon that looked like a thick bubble floating just under the sun. Through the translucent film we could see the sky, which seemed a thicker sort of blue, dreamier and closer. My mother took both my hands in hers and looked at me very seriously.

"The balloon is like the Holy Ghost," she said, "Every day our bodies pull us down. Can you feel it, Linnie? All the demons on earth try to pull us into the mundane and then we forget the spirit. We do bad things and think bad things. That's why human beings can't fly without a machine, because we are still too full of everyday badness. The balloon reminds you to always be good."

As we walked the rest of the way back to the car, my finger went numb and the pain went away. I took this as a sign that my mother and I would someday be lifted up over the wheat fields, my hand in hers, the demons far below.

The first time Lucifer tried to pull my mother away from her spiritual calling was when she was pregnant with me. She could feel him on her jaw, she said. Her mother had just died, and when the casket hit the Minnesota ground, he slithered out of it and climbed right onto her face. Whenever she tried to pray, he would grip her jaw with both hands and hold it shut. All her good thoughts about having a baby and being a mother would burn away. She felt this horrible pressure pushing down inside her until she could hardly breathe.

She stayed in her bedroom for a week, the whole congregation praying for her, and then Minister Barett, a fragile-looking man in his sixties who led the Sacred Life Church in Saint Cloud, came and talked the problem over with my father. They decided it was time for my mother to be baptized in the water again.

On a hot afternoon in August, Dee, Cheryl, and my father and mother dressed up in their Sunday clothes and drove to Lake Fairy, eight miles away from our house. Minister Barett and a few church members who knew my parents stood on shore under one of the maple trees. The day was windless and the lake was flat and green. Minister Barett read a letter from Saint Paul to the Corinthians, and then he led my mother with me inside her into the green water of the lake. My mother wore a white cotton maternity dress and went down peacefully; she didn't come up quickly. She was under water for a full minute and then the minister, who had his hand under the back of her neck and was probably tired, pulled her head back up. I imagine she thought of staying down there; maybe she thought it was the end and was relieved. When she got up from the water,

Lucifer slipped off her jaw into the lake. She watched him sink, then float away. He was upset, she said. He would be back.

While I was growing up, my mother used to drop us off at the lake while she delivered pamphlets. Sometimes she'd be gone for hours and sometimes she'd come back early and wait in the car on the bank and watch me swim. Neither of my sisters would go in the lake, even Dee, who was devoted to science and insisted there were no such things as devils, only protons and electrons. I loved to swim in the lake, especially underwater with my eyes open. In the water I would glide near the surface and flap my arms. I would dive down deep and feel the pressure of the water like a hand pushing me up. If the devil was in that lake, I wanted to see him face to face. I wanted to know where he was and study his ways so that I could understand him and prepare, so that I could recognize him when he came to our house to pull down me or my mother again.

As a child I understood perfectly why Lucifer would try to shut my mother up, to stifle her. She had a strong, wide jaw and a powerful voice. Not powerful because it was loud, necessarily, but because it carried and hovered in the air above your head. At the Sacred Life Church, where my father was minister, and sometimes in neighboring churches, she sang solos and spoke in tongues. She stood up tall, gripped the back of the pew in front of us, and spoke out words that sounded to me like harmless baby gibberish—lem lem gluk blu thout blaphlemen hulu—the small congregation leaning toward her, listening carefully. Afterward, her body dropped back to our pew, limp and soft as a newborn puppy or fawn. I suppose she could have been a famous evangelist, if she had been born a man. As it was, sincerity, devotion, and innocence in a grown woman responsible for three children was regarded as dangerous.

A few days after I'd returned home from the funeral, Dee called from her home in Louisiana. I was sitting at our kitchen counter staring at baby magazine covers and sipping hot milk to calm my stomach. I had just come back from seeing my doctor for blood test results and a checkup. Chris and I hadn't told anyone I was pregnant—we were waiting for my hormone levels to show the strength of the pregnancy. As I lay on the examining table I had tried to imagine my uterus strong and red, the fluids a lake for the fetus to swim in.

Doctor Finney's gauzy pink scarf puffed up out of her lab jacket. "It's official," she said jokingly. "You're carrying a zygote. Size of a grain of rice. Let me feel your uterus." She leaned against the table and pressed her warm hand into my abdomen, where the skin was taut and rubbery. I had gained only three pounds, mostly water, mostly in my breasts, but my body already felt adrift, slightly unfamiliar. I was thinking how the smell of Doctor Finney's underarms was going to make me heave, when suddenly my ears filled with the sound of a drum racing out of control.

"BOOM BOOM BOOM BOOM BOOM," Doctor Finney yelled into my ear and then beamed. "Next time you'll hear the heart."

I sat up and reached for my clothes. "You scared me."

On the phone, Dee's voice was dry, businesslike about cemetery upkeep arrangements, but I could tell she'd been crying. It was evening there and she was still in her office. I felt guilty that I hadn't told her about my plans and my pregnancy. I knew she had had at least one abortion. To prepare her, I began explaining how Chris and I were thinking about someday converting my painting room into a playroom.

"Why not," she said, with even more harshness than I'd expected. "If you have a kid you'll never have time to paint—you'll be too busy or too miserable."

"Some people like being mothers, Dee. It makes them happy. I think it would make *me* happy."

"There's no such thing as a happy mother. Kids are parasites depleting your electrolytes and cell salts. First you're sick all day every day and then it gets worse. You'll come home exhausted and the kid will need her pants changed, her hair combed, her nose blown, her shoes tied, an itch scratched, her tummy soothed, her face washed. She'll want less butter on her noodles, more salt on her potatoes, a hug, a walk around the block. She'll end up resenting you her whole life, and you'll end up hating her."

"Mom didn't hate us. You hated her."

Dee laughed, and I knew the story she was about to tell. Once, maybe more than once, our mother had dropped us off at Lake Fairy without a word and had not returned until night. Dee and Cheryl huddled on the shore in their towels while I floated in the middle of the lake. As the sun began to set, I heard through the water an eerie, muffled sobbing. At the time I thought it was Cheryl, who was known for her crying jags, but it was Dee. Dee's low-voiced animal wail, and then her high-pitched intake of breaths. The last time I heard her cry.

"Dee," I said to her now. "Mom couldn't help it; she was sick."

"Well, and now she's dead and can't help that either. I'm sorry, Linnie, but whatever fairytale you've got going about motherhood, you'd better get over it. There are real lives at stake—only one of them yours."

I hung up the phone and laid my head on the kitchen counter. The hardness of the wood pressed into my cheek. A tiny fly trotted across my baby magazine; it stopped in the shadow of my nose and looked up at me, the size of a grain of rice, boom boom booming toward life.

A Sunday morning in July, a month after my mother had bought me the helium balloon, Dee, Cheryl, and I sat outside our mother's bedroom door listening to her crying and talking. We hadn't heard her move for a long time, so we were sure she was kneeling, her hands folded close to her chest, her eyes closed and head raised high as if she were offering her mind to the Lord. As we listened, her voice got loud and wet, but mostly it was tiny. A whisper.

Cheryl and I sat facing Dee, who was slumped against the bedroom door with her legs propped up on the wall. She was filling in a crossword puzzle from one of her *Science in America* magazines.

"I can't hear her. What's she saying now?" I said.

Dee turned her head and pressed her ear against the door. "She's saying what she's been saying all morning, what she always says. 'Jesus help me. Jesus I love you.' I wish she'd ask him to wash and dry the damn dishes."

She looked over at us defiantly when she said "damn." If my mother had heard her she would have covered her ears. Cursing went inside her like a physical pain and I wished Dee hadn't said it, even though my mother couldn't hear her. Dee went back to her magazine and looked disgusted, but she was afraid, like the rest of us. Maybe more so, because she had been with my mother the longest and knew what she was capable of.

This was the longest my mother had stayed in her room since I could remember. My father brought her food and slept on the couch in the living room. He'd go back into the bedroom later in the morning and we'd hear him talking to her in his soothing voice; sometimes he'd read passages from the New Testament. We seldom heard her say anything back. Our father told us she was sorting things out with Jesus and that everything was fine. This morning he was giving a sermon at the church. Though my father was a Pentecostal minister and strove to preach the truth, he often did not recognize it in his own home.

Cheryl, who was ten, usually followed Dee's lead, but in the face of my mother's week-long retreat she wasn't quite old enough or brave enough to pull off her pretend disdain. "What if she doesn't ever come out?" Cheryl asked.

"We could tell her we miss her," I said.

"Brilliant," Dee said, and flicked her pencil on the magazine. "Go right ahead, Einstein, I'm sure that will bring her rushing out here."

"We could tell her we're hungry," I added.

Dee let her legs slide down the wall, got up and went into her bedroom. I heard her flop herself down on her bed. I huddled closer to my mother's door and then lay on my stomach, trying to see into the room between the carpet and the door frame. It was dark, and I imagined my mother on her knees, alone, fighting off Lucifer and worrying about who was taking care of her children.

"Mom," I whispered under the door. "We're hungry. You can come out now we gotta eat some food."

"Praise the lord!" Dee yelled from her room. "It's a goddamn miracle."

"Mom, it's Linnie. We got to cook something now or maybe we'll starve. Mom, can you hear me?"

"Oh my gosh darn dammit god. My goddamn poor children will starve to death. Oh Jesus come into my heart."

"Shut up, Dee," I yelled, and started to cry. "Don't you say one bad thing. Don't you or she'll never come out. Mom, please. Please come out. We'll be good."

I leaned against the door and begged my mother to return to us. I promised her that we would eat everything she made, that we would make our beds without being told, that we would dress ourselves faster in the morning and be quieter after school, so quiet she wouldn't even know we were there. She could read books or sew or go for walks or just sit in her chair and think.

I didn't see the knob turn or feel the door open. I was lying on my side, and looked up, and there was my mother, tall and with her hands on her stomach, smiling down at me. She looked like she had just brushed her hair and wiped her face. Her lips were sore and puffy, and she was wearing pale pink lipstick, which seems odd to me now because it would have been against her beliefs. Crouching down in the doorway she pulled me up from under my arms. She put her hands on the top of my head and kissed my cheek. She held my head in her hands, and pressed me to her shoulder, and whispered into my ear, "He didn't win, Linnie."

After I'd gotten my mother to come out of her room, she gathered us around her in the kitchen and asked us what we wanted to eat. We wanted her chocolate chip cookies, we told her. Dee said we shouldn't eat cookies for breakfast, but my mother tied her apron behind her back and took out a large metal bowl from under the sink. She opened the fridge and took out butter and eggs, then brought the big bucket of flour from the pantry. She unwrapped the butter and dropped it into the bowl, added eggs and flour, and then stood in front of the table and stared at the ingredients. The whole time she was smiling.

"What should I put in next?" she asked.

"Sugar," we said.

She pulled a two-pound box of sugar from the cupboard above the sink and started pouring it over the butter, eggs and flour. Dee made a little noise, but my mother kept pouring until the entire contents of the box was in the bowl. Then she crumpled up the carton and threw it into the sink.

"Now we mix it," she said. She took a fork and started stabbing the butter. It was hard from being in the refrigerator and there was too much sugar. We sat quietly and watched her. The fork scraped and clanked against the bowl, and bits of butter and flour and sugar flew out onto her apron, the floor, the refrigerator door. My mother's face was turning red. She took a bag of chocolate chips from the cupboard. She opened the bag, dumped the chips into the bowl.

When the dough was half mixed, she asked us what was missing.

"Salt," Dee said, and we all repeated "salt."

On the table were the salt and pepper shakers in the shape of black and white cats with big bellies. My mother picked up the salt

Heavier Than Air

shaker, twisted off the cat's head, and dumped the contents into the bowl. Dee went off to her room and Cheryl followed her.

When the cookies were done, I sat at the table with my mother and ate one. The salt burned my tongue and throat. My mother's hands were shaking, though her face was pale, calm, tired.

She picked up the fork and pushed the plate of cookies away from her. "Do you know why we have stomachs?" she asked me, and I shook my head.

"Human beings have stomachs because we are greedy and selfish and hungry for the world," she said. "But someday that will change, and where our stomachs are will be a holy, hollow place. All of our blood will go to this place, and we can walk around all day thinking about how to best save ourselves."

I sat with my mother at the table until my father came back and announced that he was taking us all to Lake Fairy for a family outing, something he often did when he sensed he'd just come home to a disaster. In the car, he patted my mother's stomach. "Little potbelly stove," he said. I remember this because my father didn't usually pat her there. He usually patted her on her back, beneath her neck, or on her shoulder.

At the lake, Cheryl and Dee hiked with my father along the water's edge while I swam near shore. My mother stayed in our station wagon under one of the maple trees close to the beach. From the water I could see her gazing out over the lake. She was turning the headlights on and off. Underwater, I imagined I could see the fuzzy track of light appear and disappear. I dove down very deep and stayed under as long as my breath would hold. I thought she might notice and become worried, but when I came up she was still sitting there.

From the water I could see her get out of the car and walk out onto the beach. My mother hadn't been in the water since Minister Barett baptized her, but she started walking into the water up to her knees. The hem of her yellow dress darkened with the water and made the skirt flatten over her belly and legs. She was pressing the heel of her hands down on her stomach.

"Linnie," she called out to me. "What do you think about having a baby brother or sister?"

I swam closer and looked up to see her eyes which were usually blue, like mine, but when she was thinking or tired they turned dark and seemed deeper set into her face. I could see she was thinking very hard and looking deep into the water.

"That'd be okay," I said.

That night when I was almost asleep, my mother came into my bedroom and lay next to me on my narrow bed. I put my arm on her shoulder; she was very hot. While she talked, I watched the lines around her mouth stretch and shrink. She was pushing down on her stomach, like she'd done at the lake, as if pushing her body away from her. "I'm afraid for my soul," she said. "I feel like I'm drowning. He's sitting on my lungs and I can't breathe, Linnie. Do you understand?"

I didn't understand, but I felt like what I said next would be very important. If I didn't say the right thing, she would leave. So I leaned forward and kissed her forehead, the way I'd seen her kiss people in the congregation. My mother was happiest when she was teaching us about our spiritual selves, and I imagined helping her teach this new baby. Later I would know that the idea of another child terrified her, but then I thought the baby would bring out the best in my mother, the tender part that loved Jesus. I imagined there must be a place where the mundane met the spiritual, and that my mother and I and this new baby could live in this place. I told her that I did understand, and that when the new baby came I would help her take care of it. Then I turned my head away from her and lay there with my eyes open and pretended to be asleep.

A few weeks after my mother's funeral, Dee sent my little maroon picture Bible she'd found going through boxes in the attic—

probably as her kind of peculiar joke. I sat down on the couch and paged through the pictures of the book. I imagined a baby floating inside me. She would look like me, and I imagined my mother sitting on the couch reading the Bible stories to her.

When I was first thinking of having a child, a few years before my mother died, I had called my father and asked if he thought she had ever really wanted to be a mother. He didn't answer at first, which surprised me. When he finally did answer his voice was sincere and light, but not phony. I expected him to say, "Your mother loved you all and never meant to hurt you." Instead he said, "I really don't know, Linnie."

In the book was one picture that showed Lucifer clearly: he was rubbery and green, just like I remembered. I could feel my upper lip sweat and I started to feel nauseated. Dee had scrawled words over the picture near the bottom of the page. "Trolls," she'd written.

That's exactly what he looked like—a goblin, a gremlin, a dragon, a grinch, a ghost. But there was nothing unreal about him. Though he spun around inside our heads, no heavier than air, he could not be dismissed. My mother and I had been plagued by a fairytale creature. As I sat there on the couch, I wondered if he would plague us forever.

As a child, I blamed the devil for everything wrong with my mother. He was upset and would be back, my mother had said, and that's why she had to stay vigilant. She was protecting us from him. That's why she burned our meals and forgot to pick us up after school. That's why she wandered outside just as we were setting the table to eat or play crazy eights with her, as we sat on our beds waiting to get our hair brushed. That's why she brushed our hair hard sometimes, and tied our belts on our dresses too tight.

Dee was the oldest; her ears and eyes were always tuned for physical disaster. I was the youngest and had to find a way to believe my mother loved us. The devil had been washed off into Lake Fairy, but he was waiting to come back; she had to pay close attention to the whispering sounds of his voice or lose us all.

That last Sunday night, after my mother left my room, I fell asleep. In the middle of the night I woke to sounds in the bathroom. I got out of my bed and passed my mother's closed door.

She was sitting on the bathroom floor, the bottom of her night-gown covered with blood. There was watery blood on the floor, and she had been wiping the blood with a towel. I stared at her, and she looked up at me like I was the mother and had caught her doing something bad. She just sat on the floor looking like a big soft baby. She reached out one hand and smiled at me. I turned on her then for the first time, the way I had seen Dee turn on her throughout childhood, the way she turns on her even now. I blocked out all my need for my mother, and fear of losing her, and love for her. I only let the hate through. I purely hated her. I saw the look on her face, guilt but also relief, and knew that she had ruined something, and that we didn't want the same thing at all.

I said what I thought would frighten her the most, maybe be-cause it would have frightened me the most to believe it. "Look what you did," I said to her. "You're evil."

The first three months she was in the home I wouldn't speak to her. She never asked for me when she was on the phone with my father. Then one day I found under my bed one of her religious pamphlets entitled "Cry in the Wilderness" and decided I wanted to see her. She was sitting on the end of her bed with a book in her hands. The room was bare and white with white curtains, no distractions, only dreamy white gauze. There were no photographs of us anywhere, only one picture of Jesus on the wall. The window was open. With-out looking up to see who it was she turned the book out to me. It was a picture of a big green lake.

After that I visited her on Sundays with my father, or I'd bicycle

Heavier Than Air

over alone. She would speak only to pray, and most of the time she didn't seem to recognize me. Once, when I was pedaling out of the driveway, she stood at her window and waved.

After the visits, I would ride my bike and sit on the banks of Lake Fairy. The evening sun would be reflected in the water. The water turned green at night, solid green, and I imagined glittering eyes laughing back at me. I cursed at the water, every word I had ever heard Dee say. I'd find big rocks under the trees and throw them into the lake.

Sometimes I lie awake and think about what it takes to be a parent, all the sheer physical and mental energy. All the faith. What could my mother's life have been if she hadn't had children? Why could she never put our salvation before her own? I stare at the dark shadows on the ceiling and feel a panic grow in my chest, weighing me to the bed, as if something were sitting on me, waiting.

Dee says the forces of matter will never outweigh the force of things that weigh nothing at all.

The last time I saw my mother alive, she was standing in a corner of her room at the home, staring out the window at a bluebird that was trying to build a nest on top of a bird feeder. The twigs the bird had brought and placed so earnestly kept falling to the ground.

"Silly bird," I said. "What will happen to its eggs?"

My mother shook her head and then she looked at me, but I didn't feel like she saw me. Her eyes were sunken and there were dark patches under them. I felt a twinge of fear in my stomach and repeated my question. She opened her mouth, but it seemed to be a great effort for her to talk.

I walked over to her and wrapped my arms around her and held on tight. I made myself a weight around her hips, as if with my body I could hold her to the ground.

Stigmata

LINDA PREVKEY closed her eyes, and her immaculate voice, a voice I'd rarely heard outside prayers, floated above the rest of our bored sixth-grade voices. The veins in her lids were the same blue as the eyes they covered. We stood in a circle at the front of our desks, reciting our last morning Act of Contrition. I imagined a halo surrounding Linda's pale face, her long white hair, and I was certain that if she were naked, I'd be able to see straight through her skin into her heart, which would not be sloppy with sin like Shelley's and mine. Linda Prevkey's heart would be as pure and clean and beautiful as the sand-ground ruby on the church chalice.

It was my last hour of school at Saint Mary's. Next year I would graduate to the public junior high, a red brick building a block away. The Vietnam War seemed to be ending, and spring was finally seeping into winter. When the bell rang, I didn't run and scream down the halls like the other sixth graders, or rip my shirt tails loose from my skirt, or fling my catechism into the trash. I walked to my desk, gathered my books, fastened my blue plastic purse over my shoulder, and followed Linda Prevkey out the door.

On the bus, kids sang the Rolling Stones and drew lopsided faces in the dust on the windows. Linda sat in the front and stared out the dirty window, perfectly still and peaceful, her silver barrette holding back her fine hair. In my back seat, I jiggled my knee against the dead radiator, thinking about how the past winter I'd often seen Linda hiking down the road past our house early in the mornings toward the Sauk River bridge. I would wander downstairs and sit in the living room, because I missed Shelley and couldn't sleep. Linda would appear in the shadowy dawn like a blurred ghost—no coat or hat even though the ground was frozen, her hair loose and flying out behind her.

She and her father had been living down the road from my family for years. Most of the time as I'd bicycle past I would only see her face pressed against the Prevkey living room window, staring up at the sky—like she did on the bus—or out at the barley field across the road from our houses. As far as I knew, no one from school invited Linda to their house. No one was invited inside Linda's house either. She had been marked early on as different, and therefore undesirable.

I'd also been marked early on—the girl who was caught with Pall Malls in her purse in the third grade; flunked gym and chorus in the fourth grade; kissed boys, and sometimes girls, behind the church in the fifth grade. Now I was the girl whose fifteen-year-old sister had been secreted out of Church Grove County because she was a slut. Like dust balls, the gossip about Shelley's absence gathered and then lingered in the town and school. I studied and ate lunch alone, sat on the swings alone.

Recently, a pack of boys had begun hiding behind the dumpsters. "Hey Theresa," they called out as I walked past, "want to have a baby with me?" I laughed at them, then ran home and cried, because, sometimes, I wished I could go off with them. The boys, I believed, had recognized something inside me, a desire they could smell, a confusion.

One day in March when I was sitting on a swing on the playground, I saw Linda standing over a dead tabby cat on the ice rink, where the boys were playing stick hockey. Kneeling bare-kneed on the ice, she folded her hands and began praying over the cat, not out loud, but I could see her lips moving. The boys who'd teased me gathered around her, and a few of them threw snowballs, mockingly called her The Saint. I stood on my swing and yelled to cut it out, but Linda calmly picked up the cat and held it against her chest, her head high and her eyes shut.

In that moment, I knew that Linda Prevkey would be raised on a cloud above this earth, where she so obviously didn't belong. I imagined that all the selfishness and desire had been burned out of her, and that she hovered above the mess and confusion of growing up.

The ten other kids on the bus who lived on our route had been dropped off one by one, and Linda and I were the last two left. I moved to sit in the row behind her. She pressed her face closer to the window. Following her eyes and the angle of her head, I tried to look at what she was looking at: she was staring at the sun, not directly, but at the place where the yellow bleeds into the blue.

"How do you do that?" I asked.

Linda glanced at me, then turned back to look out the window. I leaned forward into her seat—even in the beckoning heat of May, she wore two sweaters, one green and one white. They smelled like candle wax and church incense, and her skin smelled like the bleach in cleanser.

The bus rattled over the gravel road that led to our driveways, slowing and then halting in front of Linda's driveway. She pulled her face from the window and gathered her books.

"Linda, I need your help this summer," I said. She dropped her head and took a step toward the door.

"I have to go," she whispered.

The bus driver was watching us in her rear view mirror. Her sunglasses glared.

"You like to walk in the morning," I said. "I could walk with you. Can I meet you at your house tomorrow?"

The bus driver touched Linda's shoulder, bringing her back from wherever it was she went. She turned to look out the window, then at me again. She nodded.

My alarm rang just before the sun rose. I pulled on a pair of blue jeans, a sleeveless buttoned shirt, and my gym shoes from last year. I walked quietly past my mother and father's room. Shelley's room next to theirs was empty and the bed was made up perfectly like no one had ever slept in it, especially Shelley, who rarely made a bed. Downstairs I grabbed a green apple from the kitchen and stepped outside through the mudroom. I'd never been out this early. The dawn air was moist and clean. The sky hung dark blue, but where the sun rose it paled.

The Prevkey house was small and white and the back porch sagged. Linda sat outside her front door, on the top step, her palms pressed together around a plastic rosary. She was staring at the sunrise. She wore her two sweaters and had wrapped a long plaid scarf around her head and chin, which made me feel naked in my sleeveless shirt. I looked up into her living room window to see if her father was watching us. The curtain was drawn, with no light behind it.

In the morning the bus always picked me up first and Linda second. When she left the house, Mr. Prevkey watched her from the window, and after school he watched her climb off the bus and go inside the house. Her mother was dead and this was the reason, I was told by my mother, that he looked sad when he watched her.

She was his only child and a living memory of his wife. He was a mechanic and worked out of his garage next to the house. His eyes were large and blue like Linda's, and the square bones of his forehead and wrists made him look helpless and sad as he bent over the same old junkers lined up outside the garage day after day. He never seemed to fix anything, and I had never heard him speak. In a few years, he would close up shop and they'd move away.

I stood in front of the steps and waved my hand. "I'm here," I said.

She stood up and started walking down her driveway, her long skinny legs in thick brown winter pants. Stuffing the apple into my jeans pocket, I hurried to keep up. My legs were shorter than hers, and my gym shoes pinched my toes.

On the gravel road that led to the Sauk River, we turned east past my house. My parents' bedroom window was dark; in another hour or two they'd wake up, turn on the TV, drink coffee. Dad would read the funnies; Mom would sew. Outside, the morning light fed the freshly planted black fields. The barley shoots reminded me of little green straws reaching out from the ground, and I thought about sipping my morning malted milk through one of them.

Linda and I passed the sand pit, the Sauk River bridge, the second bigger bridge. The sun grew hotter, and I smelled the dust from the gravel road and the new manure. I'd never hiked anywhere, except up and down the halls to the principal's office at Saint Mary's, and my ankles and feet already hurt. I wondered how often Linda went on these hikes, and what exactly she got out of them. She marched silently ahead of me, white strands of hair slipping from under her plaid scarf, her rosary swinging from her side. Most of the time her eyes were on the sunrise, which was red, then pink, then orange until it burned away the darkest part of the sky.

I followed Linda onto the narrow gravel road that went up the big hill. Shelley and I had gone up the hill a few times, jumping off our bikes at the bottom of the road and pushing them up the shallow ditch. Shelley called it Death Hill. Halfway up, she'd drop her bike and lie on her back in the ditch, resting as tractors kicked gravel, and sometimes bigger rocks, down the hill, and carloads of high schoolers flew over the top.

"This hill's dangerous," I told Linda.

She leaned her weight forward and marched up the middle of the road.

A month after Shelley left, I had been sitting alone at a table in the school cafeteria, which we shared with the junior high. Peggy Schultz and two other, older girls wearing blue eye shadow sat next to me. Peggy and Shelley had taught me to French inhale one afternoon behind the aluminum shed in our backyard.

"Your sister pop that kid yet?" she asked. Behind me a group of girls in my class shifted their chairs, eyes on the back of my head.

"Wouldn't know," I lied. "Haven't talked to her."

I poked at my plate of mashed potatoes and green beans. Peggy scraped her shoe against the floor a few times, then they all stood up and sauntered away.

The girls behind me started whispering to their boyfriends on the other side of the table: I imagined they were plotting my future. I would be like these girls, their whispers said, girls whose futures swelled out of their bras, girls who everyone knew would be the next generation of whores and failures.

Father Leichen said the road to goodness was acting on complete faith and knowing how to suffer. One day in detention hall he'd put his hand on top of my head. "Young lady," he said, genuinely sad, "I'm afraid you are walking down a road away from God's grace toward permanent unhappiness."

As I watched Linda's back go up the hill, I pretended I was walking up one of those mountain jungle roads in Vietnam that I'd seen on TV. Boys fired guns across the road, I heard explosions. It was dark and windy. Halfway up the mountain I saw Peggy and Shelley and their friends, sprawled in the ditch, their faces blown off, chests caved in, guts strewn over their legs. I saw myself sprawled on the ground with them—a bad girl, a whore, a loser, a blowout, a slut, a no-good, a failure.

I shut my eyes and picked up my feet higher. In the pasture the oak leaves made a sound like palms rubbing together. Ahead of me on the hill, Linda's shoes scraped gravel. I followed the sound.

At the top of the hill I opened my eyes and breathed deeply. My tongue and throat were dry and swollen. My gym shoes were slick with sweat, and the rubber sole pinched the blisters forming on my toes. Wiping the sweat from my face on my shirt, I gazed out over the miles of green hills and trees and cows that lay ahead, and I was surprised by the beauty. Everything glowed, everything burned with color.

"Wow, beautiful," I breathed. "Is this why you walk like this?"

Linda stood with her hands buried in her sweaters and her shoulders slumped. The veins in her eyelids and under her eyes were red, but the skin of her face was moist and white.

"I don't know what you see," she said finally.

I frowned and swept my hand across the hills. "Well, this."

She gazed blankly over the pasture, then turned and started down the other side of the hill.

Later, of course, I would see it differently, but on that day, Linda seemed truly fearless, truly untouchable. I was afraid of both roads, of moving forward at all. But Linda was afraid of nothing.

That night, Shelley called collect from her home for unwed mothers. I could hear girls shouting and a vacuum howling in the background. I sat at the Formica kitchen table with my feet in a bucket of warm salt water, polishing the wooden beads of my first-grade rosary. Mom and Dad were watching the news in the living room in the dark.

"The whole world is a prison, Theresa," Shelley said. She said this every time she called. "I'm trapped inside this fat body and this kid is trapped inside me and kicking me every minute and we're both trapped inside this stupid house." She sighed. "I can't go out at night."

"Where do you want to go?"

"Anywhere. Saturn, Venus."

I wanted to tell her about my walk with Linda, the dawn, the big hill, the glowing pasture. After the hike I'd swept and mopped the mudroom and organized the closet in my room. I felt proud of myself, and determined. I also felt lonelier than before, not a sad lonely but a clean lonely ache from the top of my head to my ankles. I wondered if I would get used to it, and if Shelley would understand this feeling.

Right after Christmas dinner, the four of us were sitting in the living room and Shelley had told the family she was pregnant. I stared at the string of lights and tinsel on the tree. I had eaten half a bag of caramels and a bowl of candy corn and my stomach had started to bloat. "So I guess it's the wayward home for me," Shelley joked. My father glanced at the evening news, which flashed on bloody arms and legs of soldiers carried off on green stretchers. He looked at his shoes, rubbed his ankle, hung his hands between his knees. My mother pulled her lips tight together and ripped a loose thread off the couch, then she turned up the volume on the TV, and got up and shut the curtains.

Later, I sat on Shelley's unmade bed, while she picked up her hip hugger jeans and sweaters from the floor and dropped them into a suitcase. "It's so stupid to pack all this," she said. "In two months I won't be able to fit into any of it."

Before she left, she didn't even say she would miss me. She went to bed and listened to her radio. My mother, father, and I lay under our covers on the beds in our rooms, our hearts blown wide open.

"If I could just have someone to kiss to break this boredom, just kiss," Shelley said into the phone over the vacuum cleaner.

"There's nothing in this world like lying on the cool ground with a warm guy on your stomach."

After I hung up the phone, I pulled my feet out of the bucket and let the dingy water drip to the kitchen tile. My gym shoes had ground the top layer of skin off my toes, and two blisters were forming on the undersides of my feet. I stuck a long sewing pin into a bottle of rubbing alcohol and jabbed the pin into the blister sacks. The clear fluid drained into the bucket. I swabbed the sores, pulled on clean socks, and limped into the living room.

The curtains were drawn tight and the only light came from the TV. On one side of the room, my father dozed on his back in a recliner with an afghan tucked up to his chin. My mother was curled in a stuffed brown armchair in the other corner. She stitched hems and he dozed as soldiers jumped out of planes and slithered on their bellies through the jungle wearing green branches strapped to their helmets.

Climbing the stairs, I pressed on each wooden step until my open wounds stung. I stepped into Shelley's empty room and lay very carefully across her perfectly made bed. In her closet hung one fuzzy flowered sweater and a pair of white pants. I pulled the sweater off the hanger and took it to my room. I folded the sweater over my chair by my window, along with my own thickest sweater and winter pants.

Every morning for the next five weeks, while my parents slept, Linda Prevkey and I were the army of God marching down the gravel road in our winter clothes, past my house, over the rusty iron bridge, over the steel bridge and up the big hill. Some mornings the sun burned bright orange over the horizon, and some mornings the sky hung over us iron gray, the sun a drowning fire behind sheets of smoke. On the sunny days, Linda raced over the path; on the gray days, she marched slower and squinted through the gray.

The first weeks I followed a few steps behind her. The final week I caught up and we marched side by side.

Often while we walked we prayed—all the prayers that we'd learned at school, the Creed, the Act of Contrition, and some that Linda taught me which I would later find in old Roman Catholic prayer books. The Prayer for Lost Souls, Prayer for Wounds, Prayer for Suffering, Prayer Beseeching the Purifying Blood of Christ. The wind flattened the foot-high barley making it bow over the black fields.

While marching up the big hill, Linda and I prayed the rosary. She led with "Hail Mary full of grace" and I ended with "now and at the hour of our death." The pebbles slid under our feet, our words slid together, and the whole prayer moaned like one long note or plea. At the top of the hill I no longer saw the glowing green hills or pasture; I no longer imagined myself fated and broken like Peggy and the blue-eye-shadowed girls, or Shelley. I saw only the long gravel road that lay ahead. My sweaters grew heavy with sweat and weighed on my shoulders, and my bones and the tissue around them burned—but I was light, truly light, and I knew I was beginning to hover above it all with Linda.

One morning, after our fifth week of hiking, I finished cleaning out the shed, and stepped into the house through the mudroom. Mom and Dad were standing in their pajamas in the kitchen. The TV was off, and Mom was talking in a low excited voice on the phone. Dad listened close beside her. The baby inside Shelley had finally pushed out. She could come home. Dad went outside to change the oil in the car. I sat at the table and watched Mom pack jars of cherry Kool-Aid and ham sandwiches for each of us into a picnic basket.

"What in heavens name are you doing in all those sweaters?" she asked. "Wash your face and get some decent clothes on for the trip."

From the back seat of the car, I stared up at Linda's spot in the sky. We drove past her house, and I wondered if she was kneeling somewhere with her rosary, if she was sleeping. What did she and her father eat, did they ever watch TV or did the Prevkeys even own a TV, since the house had no antenna? The garage was open and I thought I saw her father in his long gray coveralls leaning over one of his engines.

Mom and Dad talked in chirpy little voices in the front seat.

"Your sister will be home soon," my mother chirped at me. "And then we'll all drive up to Paul Bunyan Park."

It was as if they'd awakened from a thick, dark sleep and had completely forgotten who Shelley was. She hated parks and family outings and would sulk at all the rest stops, restless and singing to herself. Dad would spread a blanket on the ground and fall asleep. Mom would set up a table in the shade, scratch at stains on the tablecloth and complain that no one knew how to have good plain fun. I would sit and feed half my ham sandwich to the squirrels and birds. Now in the car, my father tapped out a tune on the steering wheel and my mother hummed something that sounded like "Jingle Bells."

At the hospital, Shelley was propped up on pillows and asleep. Her black hair straggled over her hospital gown and into her pale, tired-looking face.

"Shelley," I said, and she opened her eyes, sweeping her hair back from her forehead. She smiled at me and motioned me to the bed. Mom and Dad stood nervously in the doorway.

"You're limping, kiddo," Shelley said.

"Not me," I said.

"Yeah you are. Looks like you're smuggling something in your shoes."

She pushed herself up and pointed to the green plastic chair next to the bed. I sat and she reached down and grabbed my knee, pulling my leg up. She pulled off my shoe, and then my sock. My swollen ankle hung in the air and my toes and the bottom of my foot were thick with old scabs and new yellow calluses. She frowned at me with her mouth open, then she looked over at Mom and Dad who were still standing in the doorway, looking wounded and helpless.

"What in the hell has she been doing to her feet?" she asked them.

"So what'd you do while I was gone?" Shelley asked. We were playing Crazy Eights in my room. Shelley had snuck up a bottle and was sipping brandy out of a plastic juice cup. My feet were raised on pillows.

"Nothing," I said. "Does the, you know, hurt?"

Shelley adjusted my pillows and offered me her cup, but I shook my head.

"First, it feels like someone's ripping you in half," she said. "Later, it's just like you've been burned down there."

My mother and father took turns carrying trays of cereal and graham crackers up and down the stairs. The days were long and gray. I started to think about Linda, worrying about whether she hiked without me, or waited for me on her front steps. Whether she even realized I wasn't behind her or marching beside her. Every day I lay at home I grew heavier, and I could feel my body ache for a sip of Shelley's brandy, or a cigarette, or anything that would make me feel forgetful and light.

One morning, before Shelley awakened, I heard a sound outside my bedroom window. I sat up and heard Linda's immaculate voice float up through the curtains.

"Theresa," she said. "Get up. I have something beautiful to show you."

She was standing in our front yard in her green and white sweaters and plaid scarf, staring up at me. Her face seemed thinner and paler than before and she seemed excited.

"Please," she said.

Outside, the July sun was gathering full force. Linda started walking toward her house and I limped behind her. At her front door, I waited on the bottom step, but she motioned me inside.

The Prevkey living room was immaculate. The walls were white and bare. In one corner sat two plastic kitchen chairs that looked like they'd never been used. The house smelled of bleach, like Linda. We walked down a dark hallway, past a closed door, and then past her bedroom. The door was open and I saw two sweaters spread out neatly on her perfectly made bed, and pictures from our catechism taped on the walls. In the hallway outside her door hung a picture of a blonde woman holding a baby and kneeling on the wine-red carpet at the front of Saint Mary's Church.

"Follow me," she repeated.

I followed her farther down the hall into her bathroom, which was clean and small. Linda pulled her soiled white sweater over her head, and her green sweater, and then she stood before me naked. She was so pale and thin, her collarbone and rib cage seemed to push against her skin. On her chest, over the place where her heart was, fanned a rash of scabs from what looked like fingernail scratches; more scratches spread across her shoulders and sides, as if she had tried to scrape off her skin. She had half-healed cuts on her forearms, and above one wrist, she had carved fresh letters: LINDA.

"It doesn't hurt," she said. She smiled at me and told me to wait, there was more.

In front of the sink, she tilted her head back, opened her palms over the porcelain bowl, and stared up at the fluorescent light above the mirror, just below the bulb, where the yellow shone on the blue ceramic tiles. On the wall above the light hung a picture of Jesus, and I realized she was holding her hands like his, open to the world, expectant, hopeful. I heard her breath go in and out and my breath go in and out. I was afraid, but also I hoped some miracle was going to happen; even then part of me believed that Linda was going to show me some secret salvation.

One of the cuts above her wrist had opened and I saw a drop of blood weep out and trail down into her palm.

"See?" she said. "Stigmata."

I saw the blood trickle down from the cut on her arm, and Linda saw it grow like a long awaited sign out of her palm. Her pale blue eyes lit up. Later that summer, and throughout junior high, before she and her father moved away, I would mostly remember how she had looked at me—like she needed me. And because I still wanted to believe in her completely, and because I didn't understand what was happening, I stared at the blood in her palm and tried to convince myself, the way a sixth grader can, that something *had* happened, that this blood was a mystery marking our futures.

"I saw it," I told her.

She put on her sweaters and walked me to the front door. The sun had risen above the barley. I walked down the road past my house, then cut through the ditch and over to the middle of the field, where I sat down in the dirt between the rows. I had imagined that inside Linda's heart was God's grace, that this grace was something you could earn, like a gold star on a paper. That once you had it you were safe.

Across the road, I could see Shelley's dark head sticking out her bedroom window. She was leaning on her elbows with a cigarette in her hand, blowing smoke rings and gazing over the field. As I watched, Shelley leaned farther out the window, until it looked like she was balancing only on her hips, and I shut my eyes and prayed.

NONA CASPERS migrated to San Francisco from rural Minnesota and is an assistant professor in creative writing at San Francisco State University. Her stories have appeared in literary journals and have received, among other awards, an Iowa Fiction Award from the *Iowa Review*, a Cooper Award from the *Ontario Review*, a Barbara Deming Memorial Grant and Award, and a Joseph Henry Jackson Literary Grant and Award. She lives in the city with her partner, cat, and little dog.